THIS BOOK IS DEDICATED TO:

*"All of the DISRUPTORS Who Are Not
Afraid of Being Uncomfortable."*

DISRUPT YOURSELF: *Choosing Courage Over Comfort, On Purpose*

INTRODUCTION

After standing on every type of stage around the world that you could imagine, I have seen it all. *Students, Professional Athletes, Teachers, Pastors, Prison Inmates, CEO's, even Stay-At-Home Mom's,* — I've learned that they all have the same things in common.

Most human beings only change and grow, when their minds are open or their hearts are broken. Most people know exactly what they need to do next, but they struggle finding the **MOTIVATION** to change. That's why I assumed, that if I wrote a book about being **DISCIPLINED** and getting **UNCOMFORTABLE**, most people would never pick it up.

As it turns out, I was wrong. Never under-estimate the power of a great story — *which is exactly what this book is, a story* — with powerful takeaways that you can apply to your life. People around the world have utilized the **DISRUPTION MODEL** in this book to make radical changes to how they live their lives, run their business and how they connect with their teams and families — *simply because of the characters in this story.*

The Division of Motor Vehicles and the hospital emergency room are two of the only places remaining where every person must visit, eventually, regardless who you are or where you're from. Those are two examples of public places where we must still learn to **connect** with others, learn to be **patient** and learn to act like decent **humans** again. That's why the DMV created a perfect backdrop, for the scenes of this story to take place.

Get ready for a message that will make you think.
Get ready, to **DISRUPT YOURSELF.**

Enjoy!
Morris Benjamin Morrison

1 *LONG FLIGHT HOME*

Miss Minnie said, "Tell Judge Fox that he must follow the rules, no exceptions. He must come in person to pick up his identification."

Unsure what to do next, Zach Gaston, the newest clerk on Judge Fox's legal team, turned and walked out of the DMV.

~~~~~~~~~~

Sitting on the airplane, Emmett Cooper glanced up from the story he was reading on his phone.

"What are you reading?" Avery asked.

"I'm not sure yet. I think my mother sent this to me by accident — she was supposed to send the invitation, but I'm not sure what this is," Emmett said, as he closed the email on his phone.

Emmett Cooper and his girlfriend Avery sat inside of the airplane at JFK airport. Their flight was delayed — which was pretty normal for JFK — with no clear understanding of why they were delayed, or when they'd be taking off.

"I'm hot, I have to use the bathroom and we've already been sitting here for almost an hour — it's going to be forever before the plane takes off," said Emmett. "Plus, we still have to connect through

Atlanta just to get to Charleston — *it's going to be a whole day of travel just to get to South Carolina!*"

"Seems like you're taking an awful long trip for a lady that you barely know," said Avery.

"I wouldn't say that," Emmett said. "I *know* Miss Minnie. Everybody knows *Miss Minnie.* Mom's has been talking about her my entire life. They have some strange connection that no one understands."

"If your mom is making you fly home from New York City in the middle of your fall semester, Miss Minnie must be one special person," Avery said.

Emmett glanced at Avery.

After Avery said that, Emmett became even more curious about the letter in the email. He was thinking to himself, *why is my mom making me fly home? Especially now, in the middle of one of my most important college semesters?*

"Wait, let me see that again," Emmett said as he searched the emails once more.

"*Claire Cooper, Claire Cooper, Claire Cooper, Claire Cooper* — wow, I sure do have a lot of emails from my mother."

"Mama's boy," said Avery.

Emmett opened the most recent email from his mother Claire Cooper. The subject read: *Minnie's Way — Dedication Event.*

His mother Claire asked him to come home for one of Clairmont's most important events — the street dedication to a lady simply known as *Miss Minnie.* The entire town of Clairmont and the surrounding Charleston, South Carolina area was anticipating the celebration of a local living legend.

Emmett said, "This is strange. For some reason, every time I open the email with the invitation for the event, another document called *Minnie Moments* keeps popping up. Mom must have attached the wrong thing."

Must be cancer-brain again, he thought to himself — even though her cancer numbers had fallen pretty low and things looked great during her last checkup.

Avery said, "Try opening the email again."

"I did. But it keeps pulling up the same thing."

Minnie Moments.

"I don't know what it is," he said, "but it looks like a story or something — it's definitely *not* an invitation."

He glanced at the first sentence at the top of the document. *Everybody knew the rules. Miss Minnie made sure of it, no matter who you were.*

"What the heck is this," he whispered under his breath.

"How would I know," said Avery.

"That was rhetorical," Emmett said, as he glanced back down at the story. *Everybody knew the rules. Miss Minnie made sure of it, no matter who you were. Miss Minnie said, "Tell Judge Fox that the rules apply to him also, no exceptions."*

Emmett looked over at his girlfriend Avery.

He said, "I don't know why my mom has it or why she sent it to me, but the email attachment is a pretty large file. It looks like a book or something. I'm definitely not reading it."

Avery said, "Emmett Cooper, will you tell me a story, please?" as she batted her eyes at him.

"Stop it, I'm not reading it."

"Seriously, Emmett, read it to me. Your mother is one of the smartest women I know. She must have sent it for a reason," said Avery.

"She probably sent it by mistake," said Emmett. "No, I'm not reading it."

Avery sat up in her seat to look towards the front and back of the airplane. With the temperature getting warmer, many of the passengers were using the flight instruction sheets to fan themselves. She raised her hand to get the attention of the flight attendant.

"Any updates on when we'll be taking off?" Avery asked the flight attendant.

The attendant said, "Sorry, nothing yet. But the captain will be making an announcement soon. Can I get you anything to drink while we wait?"

"What about the wifi, can we turn that on?" Avery asked.

"I'm sorry, that won't be available until we take off."

Avery glanced back over to Emmett as she pouted. She glanced back down at his phone.

"We don't have anything else to do," she said. "Give me your phone, I'll read the story, it's not like the airplane is moving anytime soon."

Avery grabbed Emmett's phone. With a smile on her face she did her best impression of a kindergarten teacher.

"Once upon a time, in Clairmont, South Carolina."

Emmett said, "Seriously?" as he tried to take his phone away from her.

Avery said, "Okay I'll stop. But I have to read this — I just have to — especially if it's about Miss Minnie. After all — *she is the reason* we're stuck on this airplane in the first place."

She sat up in her seat as she prepared to read the story. Uninterested, Emmett slumped even lower into his seat.

Avery kissed him on his forehead.

"Stop being a grouch! I'm going to read it to you rather you want me to or not." She said, as she glance down to begin reading the story out loud.

~~~~~~~~~~

📖 MINNIE MOMENTS

Everybody knew the rules. Miss Minnie made sure of it, no matter who you were.

"Tell Judge Fox that he must follow the rules, no exceptions. He must come in person to pick up his drivers license," Miss Minnie said.

Unsure what to do next, Zach Gaston, the newest clerk on Judge Fox's legal team, turned and walked out of the DMV.

"What kind of Division of Motor Vehicles is this," he muttered under his breath as he walked out.

"You say something?" Miss Minnie asked.

"Um, what? No, no I didn't, Miss."

"That's Miss Minnie to you, son."

"Yes ma'am," he said.

As Zach walked away, Miss Minnie glanced behind him at the next person in line.

"Next. Come on now, don't hold my line up. Have your identification ready to go please."

Everyone knew that Miss Minnie meant business. The next guy in line began to speak with a European accent.

He's probably one of the bigshots at the new Volvo plant, Miss Minnie thought to herself.

"New to the area?" she asked.

"Yes, yes I am," the man said. "I'm with the new Volvo plant that just opened."

Miss Minnie smirked. "Ummm hummm," she said.

She was always right.

~~~~~~~~~~

Back on the airplane, Emmett reached his arm over to stop Avery from reading. There was something odd about the mentioning of the Volvo plant. Emmett began to feel like he recognized the story. Instantly, he went from listening to Avery read the story to being curious about why his mother Claire Cooper emailed it to him in the first place.

"Stop reading, hold on a minute," he said, as he paused and lifted his chin to looked out of the window.

After another long pause, Avery broke his silence.

"What?" Avery asked. "Is something going on with the airplane, are we about to take off?"

"No, that's not it. Let me see that for a second."

She looked confused.

Emmett glanced down at the story.

"I recognize this story, *I KNOW this story*," he said.

"You've heard it before?" Avery asked.

"No, I haven't *heard it before*, but I just realized something. That Volvo plant opened the same year I was born. This story was over twenty years ago."

"Interesting," Avery said. "Who wrote it then? And why does your mother have it?"

"I don't know but I'm about to find out," Emmett said, as he began to call his mother Claire.

The phone continued to ring.

"Voicemail," he whispered to Avery.

"Mom, it's me. We're stuck on the flight in New York. Gonna get home much later than we expected. Anyway, I have a quick question for ya, so call me back."

Avery said, "Think about it, Emmett, we're headed to South Carolina for an event for Miss Minnie, and the story we're reading is about *Miss Minnie*? Let's at least see what this is all about."

She grabbed the phone back out of Emmett's hands. As she began to read, she teased him once more with her kindergarten teacher voice again.

"Once upon a time in Clairmont, South Carolina.... "

"Just Joking," she said.

FOR *DISRUPTORS* ONLY

Just like Emmett, most people do not like being in moments that they can not control. Something as simple as being stuck in traffic or being stuck in a room with strangers can drive some people crazy.

The difference between a random moment and an opportunity is YOUR ATTITUDE. Random moments will force you to DISRUPT old patterns of thinking — especially when others are involved — because we were created to live CONNECTED WITH OTHERS in community — that's how we learn new habits.

BE OPEN TO RANDOM MOMENTS.
There may be a bigger picture that you don't see.

Scene

2

MINNIE MOMENTS

 **MINNIE MOMENTS**

Miss Minnie had been running the DMV in Clairmont for nearly thirty years and she had her own way of doing things. Her assistant Eddie had seen his fair share of drama in that DMV over the years.

"I feel sorry for the poor kid," said Eddie.

"What *poor* kid?" said Minnie.

"Zach Gaston, the judge's clerk. You know, the one that you just kicked out of here? It's tough enough being in law school, now he's bout to make his boss mad."

"What on earth are you talking about?" Minnie asked.

"Everybody knows how much Judge Fox loves to hear the word *NO*," Eddie said.

Miss Minnie cut her eyes at Eddie.

"Don't worry about the judge — I'll take care of him. I've been dealing with Frank Fox since he was a little boy — *I can handle him just fine.*"

They looked out the window as they watched Zack Gaston approach the black, government-issued SUV that Judge Fox was sitting in.

Eddie pointed.

"Look, Miss Minnie, the kid's delivering the message right now. I can tell by his body language, things ain't going too good."

Minnie said, "Stop worrying about it. Besides, we have bigger things to worry about. We have two days until Christmas, a snowstorm coming, and we're one phone call away from the state shutting us down early today. And you *know* how crazy holidays can be around here. "

"Yeah, no telling what will happen," Eddie said.

"Child, ain't no telling who gonna walk through those doors today," Minnie said.

Eddie said, "Yep, especially since Titus Klayton is in town."

"Who told you that?" Minnie asked.

"I heard he just built a house on Daniel Island. Crazy if you ask me, I would have stayed in that warm Southern California sunshine for Christmas if I was him," Eddie said.

They both glanced outside as a small crowd of reporters started gathering — they were waiting for a glimpse of Titus Klayton, one of the world's most popular celebrities.

"Looks like those paparazzi got their cameras ready to go. Boy they sure do love TK!" Eddie said.

"His name is *Titus Klayton*. Stop calling him TK," Minnie said.

Eddie frowned when she corrected him.

"Excuse me, that's what they call him on TV."

Minnie said, "I don't understand why those reporters are here already. Titus ain't even here yet, so why are *they* here? And how in the world could they possibly know that Titus Klayton is coming to *my DMV* before he even gets here?"

"That's easy, he posted it on the internet," Eddie said. "Today people announce every move they're gonna make, *online*."

As Minnie glanced up she noticed the cameras and reporters gathering outside. "Eddie, go outside and fix my sign so those crazy folks know what my rules are."

As soon as Eddie opened the door to walk out, one of the reporters yelled, *"Pastor Eddie, Pastor Eddie."*

Eddie helped Miss Minnie manage the DMV during the week. He was also the Pastor at Calvary Baptist. Eddie noticed from time to time that some people only called him *Pastor* when they wanted something from him.

Located just outside of Charleston, South Carolina, Clairmont was the type of small town where everybody knew everybody. Clairmont was also *unknown* to the rest of the world until Titus Klayton made it famous. Actually, it was *the case against Titus Klayton* that made Clairmont a national curiosity.

"Pastor Eddie, I caught your sermon online last week. It was one of the best I've ever seen," one of the reporters said. "By the way Pastor, any chance you could tell me if TK's coming today?"

"Thanks, glad you enjoyed the sermon, but you know I can't give that information. Now come on, I need y'all to back up and make some space. Ya'll can't crowd the front door."

Eddie reached up and adjusted the sign by the door.

Minnie's Rules, the sign read.

"Big deal, I don't get it, who is Minnie anyway?" said one of the *newer* reporters.

Everyone froze. They looked at him like he was crazy.

At first no one said a word. Finally, Mendy Donner, a long-time local reporter, broke the silence.

"Who is Minnie? Did you really just ask that?"

Looking around at the others, Mendy said, "I know many of you ain't from here, but please don't do anything to get us kicked out of here — just read the sign and follow the rules."

" Just read the sign And Follow The Rules. "

Eddie opened the door to walk back into the DMV, pausing long enough to turn and give the new reporter one last look as he mumbled under his breath, *"Who is Minnie? Who is Minnie? You sure are about to find out."*

Throughout this moment, everyone seemed to quickly forget about Judge Fox and his assistant Zach Gaston, who was kicked out of the DMV. After Pastor Eddie walked away, the door to Judge Fox's black SUV opened up and everyone's focus shifted back to the parking lot as his team of assistants stepped out of the vehicle.

The judge took a long gaze towards the sky as he stretched his arms. He stopped and smiled suddenly before he started walking towards the DMV entrance.

Judge Fox said, "Team, let's make a quick, friendly public appearance and keep our voters happy."

Johnny Woods, another reporter who'd been around the Charleston area for a while, said, "This could get pretty interesting... I mean, of all the days, and all the judges. *Can you imagine what will happen if Judge Fox and Titus Klayton are here in the same place, at the same time?"*

Another reporter shouted out, "Get your cameras ready, everyone, we bout to get some money shots today!"

"No you won't. Now back up," said Mendy Donner. "Judge Fox doesn't deserve to have his photo taken. Besides, ya'll know good and well that everybody in Clairmont moved on from that story a long time ago."

"Yea, you right. But I just don't get it," said Johnny Woods. "What's the judge even doing at the *D-M-V anyway?*"

"It's the DMV, everybody has to come here eventually," said Mendy. "And with the *REAL ID* laws they just passed, you can't get around it. Celebrities, athletes, homeless people, *even judges* — everyone's gotta come in person to get their IDs. Even Kim and Kanye can't even send their personal assistants to do it for them anymore."

Johnny said, "Kim and Kanye? Are you serious?"

"Shut up, you know what I'm saying," said Mendy.

Chris Stubbs decided to jump into the conversation. He was unknown to the rest of the group as a new reporter to the Charleston area. Because Mendy seemed like she knew the most, he directed he question towards her.

He said, "Hey, I know I'm not from around here, but can someone please tell me what the connection is between Titus Klayton and Judge Fox? Why did Johnny Woods just say that things could be crazy if they both show up here at the same time? *Anything I need to know about?*"

"Forget about it," said Mendy Donner. "Like I said, Clairmont moved on from that story years ago."

Judge Fox interrupted them as he walked across the parking lot to enter the DMV.

Judge Fox was tall and athletic-looking, with a corporate-type of look about him. He wore a navy blue pinstripe suit, crisp white shirt and a solid blue necktie. He had strong presence and he looked like he just stepped out of a GQ photo session. Other than a few grey streaks in his hair he certainly didn't *look* like a judge. In his mid-40s, Judge Fox had already served Berkeley County for nearly ten years as the youngest judge ever to be elected. *He had power, he had confidence, and the worst part about Judge Fox was that he knew it.*

As the judge walked past Chris Stubbs, he recognized Mendy Donner standing next to him.

The judge extended his arm for a handshake.

"Great to see you, Mendy Donner."

She hated that he always called her by her full name. There was something arrogant about the way he said it.

Looking directly at the judge without moving an inch, Mendy looked unfazed. Finally, under her breath she muttered, *"Judge Fox,"* barely acknowledging him.

Even though the judge knew he didn't have the biggest fans in Clairmont, he was still taken back by Mendy's lack of enthusiasm towards him.

Feeling rejected, the judge pulled his hand back as he adjusted his blue necktie.

With a side grin, the judge said, "Beautiful day in Clairmont, *ain't that right, Mendy Donner,"* as he walked into the DMV.

Although Chris Stubbs was a new reporter in the Charleston area, his instincts told him there was more to the story. The awkward exchange between Judge Fox and Mendy Donner was enough to bend his curiosity. So he did what any curious reporter would do. He reached for his smartphone and he Googled the words - *Titus Klayton Judge Fox.*

When the search results appeared on the screen, he gave a quick look up towards the rest of the reporters.

As he continued to read, he stepped further away from the group. Eventually, he walked to a private area of the parking lot.

All of a sudden, Johnny Woods' comment — *what if Titus Klayton and Judge Fox were here today, at the same time* — started to make more sense.

After Chris read more of the article, he paused for a moment as he looked up at the rest of the reporters. He finally understood why Titus Klayton was such a hot news topic.

Okay now I get it, Chris thought to himself, as he put his phone back into his pocket and walked back over to join the other reporters.

FOR *DISRUPTORS* ONLY

There are very few places in public that everyone must still go. Emergency rooms, hospitals, and DMV's are places that each of us must experience, eventually. These common areas, produce COMMON EXPERIENCES that everyone can relate to.

One of the most powerful ways to disrupt yourself, is to try your best to connect to the environment that you're in. Wherever your feet are standing, try your best to be in that moment. If you practice this, you will experience more, enjoy more and learn more — you will DISRUPT OLD PATTERNS OF THINKING simply by tuning in fully everywhere you go.

Scene
3   *JUDGE FRANK FOX*

Back on the airplane, as Emmett Cooper sat with his girlfriend Avery, he became more and more curious about the story. He didn't know why she sent it and he didn't understand why his mother Claire insisted that he make the trip home from New York City right in the middle of his junior year at NYU. Film school was already hard enough and he had the biggest project of his college years coming his way — his very own feature film.

He was having trouble deciding what to focus his feature film on. This project would determine if he graduated from NYU's Tisch College of Arts with a film degree, and the deadline to submit his idea was less than a month away. If that didn't cause enough stress, he also knew what was waiting for him when he graduated from NYU — thousands of other film school grads competing for the few available jobs in the film industry.

Emmett Cooper was already feeling the pressure, and this trip home to South Carolina in the middle of the semester was a **disruption**.

Then, there was his mother's cancer. Emmett wasn't too worried about Claire Cooper though, because his mother was his hero. He'd seen her win every battle she ever fought in life. She overcame family drama and many personal setbacks to eventually become one of the youngest CEOs in her industry. Not to mention, Emmett knew that Claire was *the greatest mother a kid could ever ask for.*

"Look everyone, it's Claire Cooper, it's Claire Cooper, *THE Claire Cooper,*" he would often yell out loud when they were in public together, because of the love and affection he had for his mom.

Emmett was NOT worried about his mothers cancer. He knew she would beat it, just like she beat every other challenge she faced.

Emmett's last visit home to Charleston was just two months prior, in July. At the time, the doctor said that Claire's numbers were remarkably low and he was quite optimistic about her chances of living *Cancer Free.* So, if it wasn't the cancer, what was it then? Why did she insist on him making the trip home? Emmett wasn't sure why Claire made such a fuss over him being there for a *street dedication* for Miss Minnie.

As he sat there, he realized more and more that the hot airplane they were sitting on was not moving anytime soon. With few options and *no wifi connection,* he decided to continue reading, even though he hated feeling like he was forced to be stuck in that moment.

~~~~~~~~~~

MINNIE MOMENTS

Miss Minnie was not like most people and her DMV was nothing like others in South Carolina. Depending on who you talk to, there are many versions of stories about Miss Minnie. Some people thought she was controlling and mean. Others saw a side of generosity and kindness that was uncommon. Regardless of what you thought about her, she was the center of the community in Clairmont, South Carolina.

Miss Minnie organized coat drives, food drives and any other drive you could *imagine* — she would do anything for anyone. But her best effort of the year came at the annual Christmas feast and celebration that she organized.

She ran the Clairmont DMV for over thirty years, and some people just didn't agree with the way she did things. No matter who you were, if you lived in Clairmont, South Carolina or the surrounding area, you had to cross paths with Miss Minnie at that DMV eventually.

With just two days until Christmas, the atmosphere at the DMV was already tense because December is always a busy month anyway. There were knee surgeries, hip replacements, tax donations and last-minute family vacations — seems like people tried their best to squeeze everything they could into the last couple of weeks in December. And to do those things, people needed a current ID or driver's licenses to get where they needed to go. Not to mention, Clairmont always had the annual Christmas feast on Christmas Eve, which meant that *Miss Minnie was already on edge and she still had a lot to get done for the Christmas feast.*

The energy at the DMV shifted quickly when she glanced towards the door as Judge Fox and his team walked in.

As he walked through the front door, Judge Fox turned to Zach Gaston and said, "We have a tight schedule today. Exactly how much time we have until we need to leave here?"

Zach said, "Twenty five minutes, max. We have back-to-back meetings all day."

Judge Fox took his sunglasses off as he scanned the room.

"We'll be done in five to ten minutes, so let's make this quick."

Zach Gaston wasn't just new to the job, he was also new to Clairmont. In a purely naïve manner, he was about to make his first mistake of the day and... **take a step onto Miss Minnie's bad side.**

Looking dissatisfied and unimpressed with the DMV, Zach said, "Look at this place. It's simple, it's basic — looks like someone forgot to turn the lights on."

Zach turned back towards Judge Fox and said, "I don't want to be here any longer than we need to be."

That was *Strike One* and he didn't even know it.

" *I don't want to be here any longer than we need to be.* "

Judge Fox said, "Look over there," as he pointed to the Murphy twins, Addie and Callie. "I'm going to say hello."

"Are you sure," said Zach, as he pointed to his watch. "We only have a few minutes to be here."

The judge said, "It's politics, son — always, politics."

He approached the twins.

"Addie, Callie, so great to see you!"

"Hey Judge Fox," they said together, in perfect harmony.

The judge stepped *closer.*

Addie leaned over and whispered to her twin.

"You want me to take this one?"

"No, I've got this," Callie said, as she stepped towards the judge with her arms crossed.

Judge Fox said, "How's your dad, girls? We missed him at the Holiday party this year!"

"Sorry, not this year. Daddy's schedule is way too busy for that stuff — you know, *politics*, right?" Callie said.

Judge Fox said, "That's too bad. He's normally our top donor. I mean... what I meant to say was... *the community* really missed your daddy's support this year," he said.

Callie said, "Sure, I bet *the community* really missed him."

Noticing that something just shifted in the conversation, Zach Gaston was curious. This was the most action he'd seen since his arrival in Clairmont. He glanced towards the judge to see what he would say next.

Instead, Addie stepped in.

"Judge Fox, you should understand more than anyone why my daddy's been so busy. It's not easy getting into law school as an *orphan* — especially without political connections."

"Orphan? Law school? What?" the judge asked.

"I'm talking about AJ," Addie said.

The judge looked confused. "AJ?" he asked.

Addie looked back at him with anger.

"AJ *Klayton — Titus Klayton's little brother?*" she said.

The judge adjusted his necktie — which was an automatic reaction that he always had when he was uncomfortable.

"Oh, okay. I think I get it," he said.

Addie said, "No, I don't think you do. There's no way on earth you *get it*! You have the emotional intelligence of a ten-year-old!"

Zach Gaston interrupted, "Wow, that's crazy! We're studying emotional intelligence in law school right now!"

The judge gave Zach a sideways look.

Strike two.

Judge Fox said, "Listen, like I said, girls, please tell your dad that I said hello."

Callie stepped back in front of her sister Addie.

"Unlike you Judge Fox, my dad actually loves this town. He spends most of his time putting back together things that people like you break apart. So yes, we'll tell him you said hello."

The judge looked shocked.

Then Callie added more.

"We'll also tell Titus Klayton that you said hello. *You do know that he's back in town, right?* And guess what else: Addie's dating his son AJ!"

The judge looked confused.

"Addie Murphy? You're dating AJ Klayton?" he said.

"Yep, I sure am. Is that okay with YOU, *Judge Fox?*"

Addie and Callie gave each other a special *twins* look.

"Look at his face, Callie. He can't even comprehend that in his little brain — *a Murphy girl dating the brother of a convicted criminal,*" Addie said.

Addie reached for her phone that she had hiding in her bag. She immediately sent a text message to AJ Klayton.

*/// **TO AJ** — Keep TK away from the DMV... Judge Fox is here... not a good time :(*

As soon as she sent the message, she looked up and she noticed Miss Minnie starring directly at her.

Addie knew the rules. No phones allowed. Period.

Without the slightest resistance, Addie walked up to the counter and she handed her phone to Miss Minnie.

"Did you turn the power off? Don't forget to do that too," Miss Minnie said.

As she walked back to her seat, Addie intentionally walked past Judge Fox.

Standing almost face to face, Addie said, *"Frank Fox, I can't believe what you did to AJ's family!"*

With perfect timing, Judge Fox's cell phone started ringing. He hesitated before he answered it because he knew *Minnie's Rules* — everybody did. He failed to silence his phone and after the third ring, everyone in the DMV was staring at him.

He answered the call anyway.

As he began to raise the phone to his ear, Darla DuVernay, another DMV customer waiting for her ticket to be called, said to her boyfriend, "My God, *he is crazy!* He's really answering his phone in front of Miss Minnie?"

"Mind your business, Darla," the boyfriend said.

Miss Minnie was so focused on the awkward conversation between the Murphy twins and Judge Fox that it took a moment for her to realize what the judge was doing. When she saw him put the phone up to his ear, she snapped back into focus.

"Franklin Fox, don't even think about it," she said.

"Are you serious, Minnie?" the judge said.

"What did you call me?"

The judge cleared his throat.

"My apologies, *Miss Minnie*," he emphasized. "I'm expecting an important call any moment."

"And I'm expecting Jesus to come too," Minnie said with a scolding look.

Judge Fox said, "But I need to take this call."

"And that's your right to do so, which is another reason why I love this country so much, but in this building, you know the rules," Minnie said, as she pointed at the sign.

Miss Minnie turned her head towards Eddie, who sat behind the service counter.

"Eddie," she yelled.

"Yes, Miss Minnie?" he said.

"Did you fix my sign outside yet?"

"Sure did, Miss Minnie."

Turning back towards the judge, Miss Minnie said, "Let me get this straight, Franklin Fox. There's a big ole sign on the front door. A big sign right there above the counter, yet, you still managed after all these years to forget my one and only rule? Just how you manage to do that?"

He said, "Come on now, Miss Minnie, you know I don't mean no disrespect."

The Judge pointed his hand up in the air towards the sign. "Seriously, Miss Minnie? I mean, the world has changed a lot in the past few years, don't you think your rules are a little outdated? How long you had that sign up there anyway?"

"Well obviously, Frank Fox, that sign hasn't been up there long enough, because you still can't get it right, and you supposed to be the judge of rules and laws, ain't ya?"

Everyone in the DMV laughed, which made Miss Minnie smile too, but only briefly.

"Now, now, everyone settle dow," Minnie said. "I'm not trying to embarrass anyone in here. Let's be nice to Judge Fox."

Miss Minnie was a tough lady who was always clear about what she wanted. But at the same time, she would never let anyone embarrass another person — even herself.

She motioned for Eddie to come over.

"Eddie, help the judge out please."

Eddie placed a black storage container in front of Judge Fox.

"Here you go," Eddie said. "You know what to do."

"I do NOT have to give you my phone," the judge said.

"Oh trust me, you sure are right about that, you don't have to do nothing." Eddie said, as he smiled. "But if you don't, you know what comes next."

Miss Minnie stepped back in, "What's it gonna be, Franklin? It's your choice — you can always come back another time. We'll be open after Christmas also. So just like you tell folks in *your courtroom* during their sentencing trials, *life is about choices.* And this here's my courtroom, so make *your choice.*"

The judge looked at her with disbelief.

Miss Minnie really only had one rule in her DMV. Okay, maybe she only had one *main rule*. Some of the other rules were based on common sense that Miss Minnie expected any decent, average-functioning person to understand. **Everyone knew the consequences of bringing a phone into Miss Minnie's DMV.** If she caught you with one, you could either choose to keep your phone, and lose your appointment for the day, or you could put your phone in the black box, *on silent mode,* until your appointment was over. Either way, everyone knew that if you walked out the door of that DMV for any reason, any reason at all, you weren't getting back in that day.

Miss Minnie also expected you to *be kind* during your visit. She may have also been known to expect adults to color in the coloring books if a child asked them to. But like I said, Miss Minnie's *unwritten rules* were basically understood by everyone.

Judge Fox said, "Miss Minnie, I'm not giving you my phone. *I'm not a child.*"

"You are absolutely correct, *Franklin Fox*," Minnie said with emphasis. "You are NOT a child anymore and I'm not gonna treat you like one either. You better put that phone in that box right now or get OUT of my DMV."

After a long pause, the judge made his decision to leave. As he started to exit the DMV, he paused in the doorway long enough to look over at Zach Gaston.

Zach said to him, "I just want to remind you that if we leave this DMV today, it's going to be a long drive to New Orleans tomorrow."

The judge knew exactly what Zach Gaston meant. He quickly changed his mind as he stomped like a child towards the front counter of the DMV.

Judge Fox said, "Pastor Eddie, I'm here to renew my driver's license because I'm flying out of town for a conference in the morning and I'm the keynote speaker, so I can't miss it, so let's make this quick."

Miss Minnie jumped in front of Eddie, "What kind of business conference you attending on Christmas?"

The judge froze. He didn't say a word.

"And another thing, didn't you volunteer to do the opening prayer at the Christmas feast tomorrow?" Miss Minnie asked.

She looked suspiciously at the judge.

He still didn't speak.

"Something about your story ain't adding up, *Mr. Fox*," she said.

The Judge glanced over to Zach Gaston, then he looked back down at his watch.

Judge Fox said to Zach, "Son, how much time we got left anyway, I know we probably need to get going soon, right?"

"Nope, we're good now. We got plenty of time," Zach said with an ornery smile.

The judge looked confused.

Zach added, "Plus, I think Miss Minnie is still waiting to see what choice you're gonna make about your smart phone first."

That was Strike three.

Even Pastor Eddie laughed when Zack said that.

As Judge Fox looked with disappointment at Zach, he said, "Son, exactly when *do you* report back to law school anyway?"

Like a child throwing a tantrum in a candy store, Judge Fox pounded his fist on the counter as he grabbed a customer ticket.

Miss Minnie said, "I'm proud of you, Franklin. Now please take a seat and wait for your ticket number to be called."

"*I do not have time for this,*" Judge Fox mumbled under his breath as he slammed his phone into the black box.

Just then, a tiny little toddler walked up to Judge Fox as he sat in his chair. "*Doggy. Doggy. Doggy,*" the toddler said, as she handed Judge Fox a coloring book full of puppies.

He screamed out, "What do you want!" yelling loudly as he drew the attention of everyone.

His Assistant Zach Gaston confirmed, "I think she wants you to color some puppies with her, Judge Fox."

Everyone in the DMV laughed.

Judge Fox whispered, "Zach Gaston. *Get. Out.*"

FOR *DISRUPTORS* ONLY

Leaders are responsible for setting EXPECTATIONS *and creating* VISION *to help their teams, families and communities grow. Miss Minnie's vision as a leader was to see people connect with each other — better.*

Do you have a BETTER VISION *for how your life could be? As a disruptor, you will have the opportunity to set the rules and create moments that* BRING PEOPLE TOGETHER.

As a leader, your actions should create a higher set of STANDARDS *to live by. Your standards are what makes you stand out as a* DISRUPTOR.

Scene
4   *EXPIRED LICENSE*

Back on the airplane, Emmett Cooper and his girlfriend Avery took time reading the story back and forth to each other as they sat on the airplane. As they continued reading Minnie Moments, certain details became more interesting.

"I did not think he was going to do it," Emmett said. "I did not think Judge Fox would actually give her his phone."

Avery said, "There's no way I'm giving my phone to anybody. But seriously, does any of this seem weird to you — *even just a little bit?*"

"What?" said Emmett.

"Reading about people from your hometown," she said.

"Not really," said Emmett. "These are all people that I've heard my mom mention before — I'm just curious why Miss Minnie is so cranky — I mean, *the deal with the phones*, that seems crazy to me."

Avery said, "Maybe she wanted everyone to be more focused. I once had a creative writing teacher who swore that the greatest pathway to creativity was the art of focus."

Just as Avery said that, a Delta flight attendant interrupted her.

"I'm so sorry to bother you. I'm afraid I have a bit of bad news. It looks like the flight will be delayed longer than we thought. Is there anything I can get you while we wait?"

Emmett took a deep breath and rubbed his hands through his hair with frustration.

The flight attendant continued, "I have your connection information for you. Would you like me to help you find another connection flight into Charleston?"

"No worries, it's all good. *It is what it is,*" Emmett said.

Avery looked at the flight attendant. "We're good. Thanks anyway, we appreciate your help."

Avery glanced back and Emmett.

"Really? *It is what it is?* I thought we *both* hated that phrase?"

"We do," he said. "But it's the only thing I could think of to describe how I feel right now."

Avery said, "Anyway, as I was saying — my creative writing professor — **he took our phones from us at the beginning of class to make us focus better and he only let us have a pen and paper.**"

"Did it work?" said Emmett.

"What do you mean, *did it work?*" she said.

"Were you more creative. Were you less distracted?"

"What do you think? Of course it worked, it had to. He practically forced us, we didn't have a choice," Avery said.

Emmett's mind was still thinking about Miss Minnie and the story. He said, "Well, maybe the old lady knows what she's doing."

"Who?"

"*Miss Minnie,*" Emmett said. "Who else do you think I'm talking about?"

Avery said, "I'm just saying, nobody likes being forced to do anything — I bet Judge Fox was steaming mad. And before you ask, NO, this isn't some feminist talk that I am spewing either. Some people just don't like being told what to do. Anyway, keep reading. I want to see what the judge does without his phone because I would go crazy if I were him."

~~~~~~~~~~

 *MINNIE MOMENTS*

Mendy Donner sat with the rest of the paparazzi and reporters outside of the DMV as they waited for Titus Klayton's arrival. Out of nowhere, she began to get text messages from her team at the local CBS station where she worked.

She read the first message from her boss.

> **/// BOSS MAN –** Titus Klayton - on his way - 5 minutes!!!

Mendy's heart started jumping.

"It's game time," she said to herself.

Other messages from her team showed both *excitement and jealousy* because Mendy was already given the chance to meet Titus Klayton once in the past.

In the mix of all the messages, there was another text from her agent Dawson Dobbs.

> **/// D. DOBBS –** Call now - very important. We did it Mends!

Mendy immediately ran to her car to call him.

Dawson Dobbs was one of the best media agents in the business. If he said *it's time*, then it must be something big. Mendy was smart enough to know that when you get a message from

Dawson Dobbs, you need to stop everything you're doing to respond.

She dialed his number.

Her heart raced as the phone rang.

When Dawson Dobbs finally answered, with nervousness and a bit of fear, Mendy said, *"Is this it, is it really happening?"*

"This is it Mends — this could be the one. The suits and the top brass at Paramount want to hear your pitch," he said.

"Are you serious, you aren't joking, you wouldn't do that to me, would you?"

"Nope. I don't have the money or the time to waste telling stories — plus that's what they pay you for. Let's just say we pulled some strings with this one. If this deals comes through, it could be one big Christmas Miracle — *your Christmas Miracle, Mendy.*"

Mendy said, "This is amazing. *But why now? Why now after all of this time* — why are they finally interested in my story?"

"Have you ever heard of something called *timing?*" Dawson said. "The truth is, we never know with these things. Maybe the world wasn't ready for your project yet. With all the craziness going on with social media and the major news networks, I think they're looking for a fresh perspective."

There were always two sides to Mendy Donner — the professional and the human being. As a *professional journalist* Mendy was considered to be one of the most professional reporters in the industry. But as a *human being,* **Mendy always knew she was more than a reporter and she had an obligation to make humanity better.**

Lately, she was tired of just *reporting* stories — she wanted to *create* stories. Her most recent movie script called *The TIM Project* (which is short for *Truth In Media*) is what Paramount was interested in. It focused on corruption in the media and the responsibility to deliver media that informs and educates people. A small part of her still wasn't sure what Paramount's intentions were.

"Are you *sure,* Dawson," she said.

"Sure about what?"

"Are they really interested in *Truth In Media*?"

"Who knows. But I do know this, if you're not on that red-eye flight to Los Angeles tonight, you will never know," he said.

"Wait, tonight? What do you mean *tonight*? You mean, *tonight* — *tonight*?"

"No, *tomorrow* — *tonight*. Yes tonight! Now send a copy of your driver's license to my assistant and she'll take care of your travel details — but you need to do it now, so we can finalize everything!" he said.

Mendy could not believe it. Her moment was here. The words of her professor and mentor Michael Belmear came to mind. *Great professionals are always ready for the moment — always.*

She took a deep breath as she grabbed her driver's license to text a copy of it to Dawson's assistant. As soon as she clicked *send* on the text, two things happened — *first*, she began to hear really, really loud music around her, and *second*, she noticed that her driver's license was expired. But the loud music overpowered the moment, music that could only mean one thing — *Titus Klayton was finally here.*

All of the reporters immediately grabbed their cameras and microphones as they ran towards the entrance of the parking lot.

"What kind of car is *that*? You even seen one of those before?" one of the reporters asked.

"It must be foreign, it's gotta be foreign," Johnny Woods said.

The specialty license plate on the car read, **FR33DOM.**

"Cool license plate, I like that," another reporter said. "You know he's killing the game if he has a personalized license plate of the *front and back* of the car because South Carolina doesn't even make you put plates on the front."

Courtney "Cork" Howard, a local reporting legend in Charleston, looked back at the reporter and said, "He has two license plates for a reason. He's intentional, don't you get the point?"

"What's the point?" the reporter asked.

Courtney didn't even respond. Instead, he just looked at the reporter as if he just misspelled the word *dummy.*

As the car parked, everyone bounced with energy and anticipation for Titus Klayton to open the car door. Some of the reporters touched up the makeup on their faces, others started to clear their throats — it was game time.

When the car doors opened, you could smell an exotic scent coming from the inside. Whatever it was, it smelled delicious and his Brandon Lake music was loud, *very loud.*

Courtney Howard started dancing as he screamed over the music, *"Ummm, y'all smell that? This dude is so amazing that he has his own signature scent."*

Reporter Chris Stubbs said, "Good! He deserves it."

Earlier in the day, Chris Stubbs was the reporter who sat in the parking lot reading the story about Titus Klayton on his phone. He couldn't believe what he had read. He was still angry about *some of the comments in the article about Judge Fox.*

Chris said, "After what that judge did to that poor guy, Titus Klayton deserves to have everything he dreams of and then some."

As the reporters stepped towards Titus Klayton's car, Mendy Donner began to slowly, slowly step away from the crowd. She now had two *major things* on her plate — *her trip to Los Angeles and her interview with Titus Klayton* — which was the main reason why she was at the DMV in the first place.

Just moments after sending the photo of her driver's license to Dawson's assistant, she received a text back.

> /// **ASSISTANT** — Your driver's license is expired!
>
> /// **MENDY** — I know, I know. At the DMV checking on it now...
>
> /// **ASSISTANT** — Hurry! Or Paramount will cancel the deal!

Mendy looked towards the entrance door of the DMV, then she looked back over her shoulder. She knew that if she walked away from the rest of the reporters, she would NOT get her opportunity to interview Titus Klayton again.

She looked at Courtney Howard.

"Hey Cork," she said, "get my back on this one and I'll get you next time?"

"Sure Mends, what do you need?"

"Can you convince Titus Klayton to hold me a spot for an interview next week? If anyone can pull it off, you can!" Mendy said with a smile.

"What? *A one-on-one, seriously?*" Cork said.

"Cork, my plans just changed, I need to go into the DMV because my drivers license is expired, but my boss is going to kill me if I lose this interview with Titus. So I need to come back with something bigger — I need an exclusive interview," she said.

"Hold you a spot? You've been waiting all morning, why would you leave now?"

"Remember my *Truth In Media* Project?" she said.

"Yeah, that *TIM thing*, right?" he said.

"Yes, that *TIM thing*."

Cork said, "Still trying to speak truth to power, I see?"

She said with excitement, "I literally just got the call so I gotta get to LA now, Paramount wants to hear my pitch."

"Are you serious? Paramount? That's amazing!" he said, as he jumped to give her a hug.

"Yes, dead serious," Mendy said. "And Titus Klayton already knows about the project because I started writing him years ago when he was in prison about the media's negative influence in our culture, so Titus should be pretty excited for the interview!"

"If anyone wants to see changes in the media it would be Titus," Cork said. "I will see what I can do. Okay go. You better get into the DMV to take care of business and pray that Miss Minnie doesn't stick it to you. *Two days before Christmas* — it's a madhouse in there."

Mendy rolled her eyes and smiled. "Trust me," she said, "the only person I'm thinking about right now is Miss Minnie. I hope she takes it easy on me. Hopefully I'm in her good graces because our company sponsored the Christmas feast this year."

She hugged Cork with appreciation.

"You're the best, wish me luck," she yelled as she hurried away.

"When you walk in that door, you're going to need more than luck," Cork yelled back. "It looks like Judge Fox has already made her mad today, so be careful."

FOR *DISRUPTORS* ONLY

Disruptors understand how to use their POWER and INFLUENCE to impact the world around them. If you are reading this book right now, there's a great chance that you're already aware of your ability to make a difference in the lives of others.

Disruptors are always one step ahead. Simply understanding your power to influence is the first step. The next step is to PUT YOUR POWER INTO ACTION by using your gifts, to lift up the community around you. Because Disruptors never "disrupt" things for selfish gain. They do everything they can to MAKE OTHERS around them, BETTER.

Scene

5 *DARLA DUVERNAY*

MINNIE MOMENTS

"Darla DuVernay, Darla DuVernay — come to the counter please," Miss Minnie announced.

As Darla DuVernay made her way to the counter, she accidentally bumped into Mendy Donner, who was walking through the front door of the DMV.

After she recognized it was Mendy Donner, her head sunk deeper into her chest. Darla could barely make eye contact with Mendy. Somewhere between her lack of self-confidence and the fact that Mendy Donner was a local celebrity in the Charleston, SC area, Darla felt embarrassed around other powerful women.

"Here, let me get that for you," Mendy said as she picked up Darla's paperwork that fell to the floor.

"See, all good now," Mendy said.

Still barely able to make eye contact, Darla whispered, "I'm sorry I got in your way," as she made her way to the counter to see Miss Minnie.

Got in my way? Mendy Donner thought to herself.

Something about the interaction made Mendy Donner uneasy. She never wanted someone to feel sorry for *getting her way*. **As a journalist she viewed herself as a servant. The last thing she wanted was for people to think that she was unapproachable.**

"Is this yours too?" Mendy said, as she handed Darla an ink pen that she dropped.

Mendy extended her arm to shake hands.

"I'm Mendy, what's your name?" she asked.

Before shaking Mendy's hand, Darla DuVernay glanced over her shoulder at her boyfriend. The boyfriend gave a look that clearly showed he was uneasy with the interaction.

From a distance, he tried to quietly yell, *"Hurry up, let's go,"* as he motioned with his arms in the air.

Miss Minnie was waiting for Darla at the counter. For some strange reason, Miss Minnie always showed Darla extra grace and compassion. Even Darla couldn't understand why Miss Minnie treated her so well.

Minnie treated a lot of folks well, but if you acted out of line, as people often did at the DMV, you'd get a chance to meet the *other* side of Miss Minnie.

As Darla approached the counter, Miss Minnie dropped the pen and paperwork that she was holding as she stopped everything to greet Darla.

Pastor Eddie was standing beside Miss Minnie.

"What are you doing?" he said.

Miss Minnie said, "Eddie, can't you see that one of my favorite people in the whole world is here?" as she stepped around the counter to hug Darla.

Other customers at the DMV stopped to watch. It was rare to see Miss Minnie show affection like that, to anyone.

As she hugged Darla, the extra attention from Miss Minnie and from the other customers watching her was enough to make Darla want to run and hide.

"*Darla DuVernay, Darla DuVernay* — it is just so good to see you," Miss Minnie whispered in her ear as she hugged her.

"Hi Miss Minnie, good to see you too," she whispered back.

"It's always so good to see you, my Darla DuVernay," Minnie said.

Whispering at a low volume, Darla said, "*Why do you still call me that name?*"

"Told you that once already, no need to say it again," Miss Minnie said with a smile. "Now… *let's talk about more important things,*" Minnie said, as she glanced down towards Darla's stomach.

Darla's whole body froze.

Miss Minnie looked into Darla's eyes. After pausing long enough, she glanced back down at Darla's stomach. "Didn't think I knew about the baby, did ya?" Minnie said. "How far along are you?"

Still frozen, Darla didn't speak a word.

Before saying anything to Miss Minnie, she glanced over her shoulder towards her boyfriend. They hadn't told anyone else that she was pregnant.

How does Miss Minnie know? Darla wondered.

With his arms crossed, the boyfriend starred back at Darla from across the room with a disapproving look.

Miss Minnie said, "Well, you can stand there quiet as a mouse if you want to, you don't have to say a word."

Darla looked shocked and amazed.

"You're probably wondering how I know," Minnie said.

Still unwilling to confirm Miss Minnies suspicions, Darla leaned a little closer to Miss Minnie.

"*How exactly did you know?*" Darla asked.

"Child, you look happy, *on the inside.* You couldn't hide that glow from a mile away," Miss Minnie said with both of her hands softly holding the cheeks of Darla's face.

Darla said, *"But... I... I didn't..."*

Minnie interrupted her as she leaned in to whisper in Darla's ear. "Your whole life just changed. The question is, what you gonna do next? What's the plan?"

"I don't, I mean... we don't." Darla stopped talking.

"At least tell me that he's treating you right?" Minnie said as she turned to look at the boyfriend — giving him a look of death from across the room.

"But how did you know anyway?" Darla asked.

"Just doing my job," Minnie answered. "And don't you forget why I nicknamed you Darla DuVernay. She was one of the greatest women I ever knew, and that's what you are, great. You are going to do amazing things in this world one day, you understand me, child?"

"And that's what you are, great.
You are going to do amazing
things in this world one day."

"I guess," Darla softly answered.

After grabbing her paperwork from the front counter, Darla returned to her seat. Her boyfriend watched the whole interaction from the other side of the room, but he couldn't hear everything that was said.

"What's the deal with that Minnie woman anyway? And why was she looking at your stomach? What did you tell her?" the boyfriend asked.

"What?" Darla said. "I don't know."

"Then what was all the talking about?" he asked.

She said. "You saw the whole thing, I barely said a word."

"Doesn't matter anyway," the boyfriend said. "It's gonna be handled soon anyway, ain't that right?"

Darla looked back at him without responding, as she glanced back up towards Miss Minnie with both of her hands gently rubbing her belly.

Darla noticed that Mendy Donner and a few others were watching her interaction with her boyfriend. Mendy heard the boyfriend's comments to Darla, and everyone knew exactly what he meant. Mendy folded her two hands together as she gestured in Darla DuVernay's direction, a gesture that seemed to communicate the words *I'm praying for you* from the other side of the room.

~~~~~~~~~~

Back on the airplane as Avery and Emmett took turns reading the story, Avery became much more emotional after the exchange between Darla DuVernay and her boyfriend.

"Can you believe that guy," Avery asked. "The thought of him even *thinking* about forcing Darla to do that, I could smash this phone on the ground right now it makes me so angry."

"What?" Emmett asked.

"What do you mean... *what*?" Avery responded.

"Why are you mad at the boyfriend?" he asked.

"Because, he obviously doesn't want her to keep the baby!" she said.

"Wait, hold on, don't you think that's a stretch? What makes you think he doesn't want the baby?"

"You saw what he said. We're gonna TAKE CARE of it soon anyway! That only means one thing," she yelled.

Their conversation was interrupted by Emmett's phone as it began to ring.

"Here, it's your mother, she's calling you back," Avery said.

As Emmett attempted to answer the phone, he knew that cell reception on the runway at JFK airport wasn't the best, but he tried his best to talk to his mother Claire.

"Mom. Mom. You there?" he asked.

"Emmett, Emmett, how is your travel? Will you be on time tonight? Emmett can you hear me?" Claire asked.

"Yes Mom, I can hear you," Emmett said. "Hey Mom, I hope it's okay, but I wanted you to know that I'm reading the story that you emailed."

"What did you say Emmett? Say that again," she yelled.

"Mom, I'm reading the story that you emailed me, *Minnie Moments*. I'm reading it now. Hey, what's the deal with this story anyway?"

"What story? What are you talking about?" Claire said. "Emmett, I can barely hear you. Are you there?"

"The story you emailed earlier today, Avery and I are reading it now."

Claire interrupted. "Emmett, it sounds like you're still on the airplane, but I can barely hear you. Miss Minnie's dedication event starts at 7:00pm tonight. You chose a same-day flight even though I told you not to, so you better not be late!" she yelled.

Emmett and Avery looked at each other. The cell phone reception was bad, but both of them clearly heard the point of Claire's message — **don't be late tonight.**

As the cell reception continued to break up worse, Emmett decided to end the call.

"I'll just call her back during our layover in Atlanta," he said.

FOR *DISRUPTORS* ONLY

If you want to show another person respect, give them your full attention. Giving someone your full attention communicates three powerful words that every person wants to know – I SEE YOU.

Disruptors are aware of their IMPACT ON OTHERS. *The more you learn to show genuine excitement when you talk to another person, the more you will develop greater respect for yourself.*

Disruptors know that their energy and presence can either lift people up, or push people down. Always use your presence to LIFT OTHERS UP.

Scene

6

FR33DOM

 **MINNIE MOMENTS**

The audience outside of the DMV began to grow larger and larger as they waited for Titus Klayton to get out of his car and enter the DMV.

"What's going on? Why is he taking so long?" one of the reporters asked.

"How would you like it if every move you made was being recorded?" Cork Howard yelled. "Let the man take his time."

The windows of Titus's vehicle were tinted for privacy, which only added to the curiosity of the reporters. Eventually, each of the doors to the vehicle opened at the same time.

AJ Klayton, Titus's younger brother, was the first to exit the car.

"Guys, I'm sorry to be so tough on you today, but I'm going to have to ask you to step back," AJ said. "Please step further away than usual, and absolutely NO photographs at all today."

"What, no photographs? Who does the guy think he is? I'm taking pictures, it's my job," yelled a random reporter.

Screaming over the loud music that was still playing, AJ said, "Excuse me, what did you say? I couldn't hear you."

The reporter said, "Well maybe if you'd turn your music down, Mr. DJ, we could all hear a little better. What kind of music is that you're listening to anyway, some new type of bippity bop?"

AJ couldn't hear what the reporter was saying, but based on his body language, he could tell exactly what the reporter was *trying to say.*

As he approached the reporter, AJ said, "Listen man, I don't know what you just said, *but like I said,* no photos today. Please show some respect."

"Respect? What?" the reporter said.

Feeling challenged, AJ immediately stepped closer to the reporter. Just as he began to speak, a tiny voice yelled out from the car.

"Uncle AJ, Uncle AJ, you promised to find my favorite song."

Immediately stepping back towards the car, AJ said, "Hey babygirl, Uncle AJ's right here. What do you need?"

"I can't find my Kidz Bop song and I'm sad. You promised you'd help me find it."

Another tiny voice from the other side of the car yelled out, "No Dori, it's my turn to pick the song," as she ran around the car to argue her point to Uncle AJ.

AJ said, "Gabby, Uncle AJ has to help your sister first. I promise we'll get to your song in a minute."

After noticing the presence of the two little girls, reporter Johnny Woods began to motion for the other reporters to step away from the car.

"Come on now, this ain't Hollywood," he said. "Y'all know how we do things in South Carolina. No photos of kids and families. Now back up and show some respect."

Cork Howard said, "Yep, I saw ya'll dancing to that new music — and you liked it too! No cuss words, dope beats and great energy, that Kidz Bop ain't no joke."

AJ Klayton immediately smiled when he noticed Cork.

"Cork, my man. Good to see you bruh!" he said.

As they began to embrace, AJ said, "Cork I'm glad you are here. Finally, someone I can trust — hey can I ask you a favor."

"Anything for you, what you need?" he asked.

"Is Judge Fox still in there?" AJ asked.

"Unfortunately, he is," Cork said.

"Listen, I'm trying to eliminate as much drama today as possible. Can you please help us get in and out of here as fast as possible?" AJ said.

"Sure, you know I've got your back," Cork said.

"Please ask the other reporters to stand down," AJ said. "Titus will give them all the interview time they want, but just let us get in and out with Gabby and Dori first, then he'll handle the interviews, okay?"

"No problem," Cork said. "Plus, I bet Titus Klayton will have a lot to say when he comes back out of the DMV anyway. Has he even seen Judge Fox face to face since he came back?"

"Fortunately, no. But that's about to change. They'll be seeing each other today and tomorrow," AJ said.

"Tomorrow?" Cork asked.

"Yeah. The Christmas feast. Titus is speaking at the event. I heard that Judge Fox was supposed to give the opening prayer too."

Cork quickly opened up the calendar on his phone.

"Yep, I'm glad it's already on my calendar. I can't wait to see how that plays out," he said.

"Yep, who knows what will happen," AJ said.

Turning towards the car, with a smile AJ said, "Okay, I'm going to see if Titus is ready to make his entrance."

As AJ walked towards the car, Gabby and Dori began to argue.

Gabby said, "It's my turn, Dori."

"No, you helped daddy last time," Dori said.

"No, Dori, you pushed him around the toy store today."

AJ interrupted. "How about both of you. You can both help your daddy today."

"Both of us?" Gabby questioned. "How we gonna do that?"

"By being nice to each other, that's how," AJ said.

As AJ opened the passenger side of the car door to help his older brother Titus out of the vehicle, Titus Klayton's bright smile began to light up the parking lot — a smile that shook the consciousness of the on-lookers to their core. Titus's presence was so strong that, oftentimes, he distracted on-lookers from the presence of his wheelchair.

After helping Titus into the chair, AJ turned to glance in Cork's direction to remind him of their deal.

"You ready, Cork, you got me?" he asked with a nod of the head.

As they turned to watch AJ push Titus's wheelchair into the DMV, the group of reporters and other members of the paparazzi got a glimpse of humanity that was rare to see with their cameras covering their faces. But today, in an act of respect and solidarity, everyone smiled and cheered Titus on as he wheeled past.

"Daddy, Daddy, I forgot my toys in the car," Gabby said, as she tried to step back towards the car. "Uncle AJ, can you unlock the car door for me pleeeeeeeease?"

Titus interrupted. "Gabby, I'm sorry sweetie, but you aren't allowed to take anything into the DMV with you," he said.

"Why not, Daddy, it's just a toy?"

"Because those are the rules," Titus said.

Dori chimed in. "What kind of silly rule is that, Dada?"

Titus looked up at his brother AJ as he smiled.

"Honey, it's called Minnie's Rules, which is something you're about to learn for yourself," Titus said, as he gave AJ a fist bump.

"Sorry, girls. It's a rights-of-passage that everyone in Clairmont must experience. And today, it's your turn," AJ said.

"Rights-of-passage?" the twins said in unison, looking at one another. "What is that?"

FOR *DISRUPTORS* ONLY

If you knew the backstory of another person and you understood the challenges they had to overcome, you would have a different opinion of them.

Disruptors take time to BUILD RELATIONSHIPS *with others instead of judging them.*

We PROJECT *our own fears and insecurities onto others. So next time you decide to judge another person, stop to ask yourself why. Because your feelings may have nothing to do with the other person, and everything to do with* HOW YOU SEE YOURSELF.

Disruptors TAKE TIME TO GET TO KNOW OTHERS, *instead of judging others. This will allow you to disrupt old mindsets and grow. It's also a much better investment of your time and energy.*

Scene

7

TEN STEPS AHEAD

Back on the airplane, Avery and Emmett both sat with stunned looks on their faces. Neither of them knew exactly what to expect as they read the story.

"There is no way I would have imagined Titus Klayton being in a wheelchair," Emmett said. "What do you think happened to him?"

"I don't know," said Avery. "The whole time he sat in his car in the parking lot, I couldn't wait for him to get out and go into the DMV — especially with the Judge Fox thing."

"I know, me too," said Emmett.

Emmett was always obsessed with the art of storytelling. His whole reason for going to Film School at NYU was to learn how to creatively tell better stories. As he read *Minnie Moments* his brain couldn't shut off the things he learned in the classroom. As he added up all of the details about the story up until this point he came to his own conclusions.

"Drama and conflict — there needs to be more conflict in this story," he said to Avery.

"Why do you say that?" she asked.

"I mean think about it," said Emmett. "The setting of this story takes place at a DMV in the country south. The DMV is run by an old lady who's determined to enforce her rules. You've got a Judge that seems sketchy, reporters like Mendy Donner and Cork Howard, Titus Klayton who everyone obviously loves, and then there's the mention of the *pregnant girl,* Darla DuVernay."

"Yes, so what about it?" Avery asked. "Every story that's ever been told had different characters."

"Yeah, but whoever wrote this story must have had a reason for each of these characters, otherwise it's all just random information," he said.

"Whoever wrote this story must have had a reason for each of these characters."

"Unless... " Avery said.

"Unless what?" Emmett demanded.

"Unless the story isn't random. Maybe it's not even fiction. Maybe the story is true — did you ever think about that? If that's the case, then the characters are who they are. *Maybe it is what it is,*" Avery said as she elbowed Emmett with a smile.

"Oh, you're a comedian now," he said.

"Like I said, Emmett, your mom is one of the smartest ladies I've ever met. There's a reason why she has this story," Avery explained.

He said, "I'm sure it has something to do with Miss Minnie's dedication event tonight."

Suddenly, Emmett reached for his phone once again.

"What are you doing?" Avery asked.

"Cell reception is bad and I can't call her to talk, but I can try to text her. The storyteller in me needs to know what this is all about," Emmett said.

He began typing the message to his mom.

> /// **TO GMEVER** — Hey!!! Not sure if txts r wrkn. Txt bk if u get this…

After he sent the message, Emmett noticed the dots on his phone where his mother was typing a response.

"Look, the dots popped up," he said as he showed Avery his phone. "She's typing something back. The text must have worked."

He immediately started typing his next message to her.

> /// **TO GMEVER** — Wasup w/the story u emailed? MINNIE MOMENTS… anything 2 do w/ 2nites event????

He began to yell at his phone, "Wait. Mom. What are you doing?"

"Look." He said to Avery. "Her dots went away. Why would she start typing a response then stop?"

"*Patience Daniel Son*," Avery said.

As they continued to wait longer and longer for Claire Cooper to respond, it was clear that either the messages weren't going through, or Claire just wasn't answering.

"Okay, Mr. Drama and conflict," Avery said.

"What?" yelled Emmett, with frustration.

"Don't just sit here," she said. "Let's keep reading to see if you're right about the drama — at *least we know that Titus Klayton and*

Judge Fox are in the same room now — there's definitely going to be some drama there."

~~~~~~~~~~

 **MINNIE MOMENTS**

Emmett realized that the story he was reading occurred over twenty years ago. He had *no idea* who it was written for. But… he knew that those people in the Clairmont DMV were in the middle of one of the most powerful moments of their lives. It probably took years for whoever wrote it, to put the actual experience into words. There were multiple characters, with different needs and complex situations. Emmett could only imagine how amazing the actual moment was because it was beginning to become very obvious to him that many people's lives were changed that day because of Miss Minnie and the others who happened to walk into that DMV.

Yes, Miss Minnie was a complicated person to some, but the truth is, she was a very simple person, who had a simple vision for how easy life could be when people just talked to each other.

" *She was a very simple person who had a very simple vision for how easy life COULD BE if we just talked to each*

She was also a *really focused* person. The reason why Miss Minnie was so focused was because she felt *called* to do her job well. She felt called to make a difference for others. She knew what God put her on this earth to do and she wasn't willing to change that, or change her rules at the Clairmont DMV, for anyone.

After many years went by, many people went in and out of that DMV. For most people it was just another transaction, something on their to-do list that needed done. And for others, it was bigger than that. It was *transformational,* because that's how Miss Minnie was — she *transformed* everything. **She thought ten steps and ten decades further down the road than most people —** *she had vision.*

"She thought ten steps and ten decades further down the road than most people — she had vision."

That's why she kept her rules no matter what, no matter who your were. She did everything on purpose, and for a reason. Some people complained about Miss Minnie, but others were blessed by Miss Minnie, if they paid attention to what she was trying to do.

Think I'm lying to you? Well, understand this — there were people who left the DMV that day and because of what they experienced, they became better human beings. Some were even blessed enough to become better mothers, better fathers, better leaders — some even found the courage inside themselves to start their own businesses. A few people even got saved after that day was over.

FOR *DISRUPTORS* ONLY

The two most powerful words that a person can say are... *I* **DECIDED.** Once a person says those two words, all of the ideas, resources and courage that they need will immediately be within their reach. And that day at the Clairmont DMV, several people **DECIDED**... to choose **COURAGE** *OVER* **COMFORT** and they learned how to **DISRUPT THEMSELVES** to become free, independent thinkers who lived *on purpose*.

That... is what really happened that day. Now that you have a better understanding of why their lives were changed, there's one more character that you have to meet — *Dorian Banks.* Dorian and his family played one of the most critical roles in the message of this story, *especially Dorian's son, Jordan.*

DORIAN BANKS

Dorian Banks was a local legend in Charleston, South Carolina. After losing his parents early in life to a car accident, Dorian developed a level of purpose, drive and determination that was rare to see at his age. He gave his life to Christ as an early teen, he was a leader in his church and school and he was a star athlete who later led Clemson University to a national championship in *basketball* — while also playing *football* for Clemson.

After a career in the NBA, Dorian moved back to Charleston to plant his roots as a family man and continue his career as a corporate executive, but the most important thing in Dorian's life was his family. He loved his wife Lisa, his son Jordan and his daughter Jeniya more than anything.

Jeniya was one of the sweetest *"Daddy's girls"* you could find. And his son Jordan absolutely worshiped the ground that his father walked on.

Dorian's role as a global supply chain leader with Boeing required much travel. When he was at home, the daily meetings and conference calls kept him away from his family more than he wanted. His kids craved any attention and opportunities to be with their dad they could get, so when Dorian offered to take time away from work to take Jordan to get his driver's license, Jordan was excited!

When they got into the car to drive to the DMV, Jordan immediately started shifting gears and playing with all of the settings in the car.

"Dad, which one?" Jordan said. "Which drive mode should I choose, *sport or comfort?*"

"Well," said Dorian, *"since I'm the one driving,* why don't you let me worry about that. Let's just cruise and relax a little bit."

"See, Dad, that's why you need a son like me. You never give these cars what they need. You need to *drive* these babies," Jordan said.

Dorian always did have the coolest cars, and Jordan couldn't resist the temptation to unleash them on the road.

"Yep, Dad," said Jordan. "I guess I better get used to this car A.S.A.P., because once I get my driver's license today, you'll need to show me how to use every feature and every button!"

"I wouldn't spend too much time studying *this car*," Dorian said. "This car is nothing like the car that you'll be driving. As a matter of fact, no one promised you that you were getting a car anyway!"

Dorian's smile said it all — of course he couldn't wait to bless his son with his first car.

"I don't care, I'm a patient guy," said Jordan. "At least I get to take my driver's test today in one of the most modern cars ever made. This thing has cameras all around it. I'm guaranteed to pass my test, and when I do, *you know what that means*."

Jordan stared at his dad with a silly grin.

Unable to resist his silly face, Dorian laughed on the inside, but on the outside, he didn't respond.

"Dad, did you hear me? I said… when I pass my driver's test today, you *know* what that THAT means, *right?* It's going down tonight!"

"Yes, Jordan. I know." His father said with relief.

Jordan said, "Go ahead dad, say her name!"

"No Jordan, please leave me alone and let me drive."

"Dad, you don't even remember her name, do you? Come on Pops, you know she's my one and only love!"

"My God, Jordan, how could I NOT remember her name, you've been saying *Sophie, Sophie, Sophie* in your dreams when you fall asleep at night."

"Dad, stop it. You're exaggerating."

"Don't get too cocky yet, son, you still have to pass your driver's test first. And… hold on a minute. Correct me if I'm wrong, but are you telling me that Sophie agreed to go on a date with you *tonight, tonight,* and she agreed before you even passed your test?"

"Dad, why are you hating on me right now? Of course she is going with me. Now, I just need to get in here and rock this drivers test, so God can bless the rest."

Dorian said, "Don't bring God into your Sophie fantasies, son," as he reached over and nudged his son with his elbow while giving him one of those *dad smiles*.

"I'm just playing with you," Dorian said. "Relax, Jordan, you'll do great on your driver's test! I just can't believe you're old enough to drive anyway."

"Stop it, Pops, not this lecture again."

"You'll see one day, Jordan, it goes by fast."

Dorian punched his son in the arm again as he said, "Seriously, Jordan, I am so proud of you — I love you, son."

"Of course you do, look at me," Jordan said with a smile.

Dorian said, "Nope, that's not good enough. You know what I want to hear, so let's try this again. I said, *I love you son*."

"Right back at you, Dad."

"Right back at me? Boy you better give me more than that before we go into this DMV, or I will embarrass you in front of all these girls when we get in there," Dorian said.

"Pops, chill. You know I got love for you," Jordan said, as they both laughed and pulled into the DMV parking lot.

FOR *DISRUPTORS* ONLY

Miss Minnie was a VISIONARY LEADER. *Her values reflected a desire for humans to live better.*

What are your TRUE VALUES? *Taking time to ask yourself tough questions about who you are will change your life faster than anything else.*

Two of the most powerful words are, I DECIDED. *What major decisions have you made that influenced your life the most? Remember, choices will change your day, but* DECISIONS WILL CHANGE YOUR LIFE.

Scene

8

IT MUST BE CHRISTMAS

MINNIE MOMENTS

When Dorian Banks and his son Jordan arrived at the DMV, the final piece of this story began to take place. Their presence at the DMV took this story in a whole other direction. Like all stories, anytime another character walks into a room, no matter how many people are already there, the moment someone new walks in, their presence completely shifts the room. That's exactly what happened when Dorian and Jordan Banks walked in. Things changed at the DMV the moment their car pulled into the parking lot.

Reporter Johnny Woods tapped Cork Howard on the shoulder when Dorian and Jordan got out of the car.

"Are you kidding me?" Johnny said. "You telling me that Dorian Banks is here too? This day is getting more and more interesting."

Cork made his announcement across the parking lot as Dorian and Jordan approached. "My man, DB, great to see you. And Jordan, little Jordan? Is that you all grown up like a man?"

Dorian was close enough to embrace Cork with a hug.

"So good to see you, Cork. How you doing, how's the family these days?" Dorian said.

"It's busy, DB, just so busy. And you know how my wife is, you've known Tracey since you were a kid. She's the boss and she keeps us all in check," Cork said.

"Please give Tracey my best," Dorian said.

"Will do. Hey, just so you know," Cork said, "we already have an all-star cast inside the DMV today, and now that you're here, the plot is about to thicken."

Jordan and his dad both laughed.

Dorian Banks was world-famous and he was used to attention. So at first, he brushed the comment to the side and he said hello to the other reporters as he passed by.

"Can I grab a quick comment on the record before you go?" Johnny Woods asked Dorian.

Dorian said, "My sports days are over, I have nothing to comment about! I'm a regular family man now — unless you want me to comment about my honey-do list or which grocery stores have the best produce?"

Jordan added, "By the way, Mom's going to kill you if you forget to take the trash out again."

"Trash? Trash?" Dorian asked, as he looked at the rest of the reporters. "Fellas, I need y'all to get my back here for a minute. Please explain to my son Jordan what happens on trash night, *after* a kid gets his driver's license!"

Cork Howard and Johnny Woods both laughed.

"You want to drive a car someday, right?" said Johnny.

"No doubt!" Jordan responded.

"Ummmm, yeah," Cork said, as he looked down at his watch. "Sorry to tell you, Jordan, but your dad's trash days will be officially over in about an hour."

Looking young, dumb and paranoid because he obviously didn't understand, Jordan said, *"What? What's my driver's license have to do with the trash at my house?"*

"You've got a lot to learn, Jordan," Johnny said, as he turned his attention back to Dorian.

"But seriously, Dorian, can I get a comment on the record before you head in to the DMV?"

"Sure, about what?"

"About Titus Klayton," Johnny said.

"What about Titus?" Dorian asked.

Cork and Johnny looked at each other.

Cork stepped in. "Dorian, Titus just moved back to town."

Jordan *immediately* got excited.

"Dad, I didn't know that Uncle T was back? When can we see him, when can we see him?"

Dorian's body language shifted enough for them to notice.

Cork said, *"You did know that he was back in town, right?"*

Dorian said, "Actually no, no I didn't. I haven't spoken to Titus in a long time."

Dorian's comment caught Cork and Johnny by surprise.

"Hey, you guys used to be unstoppable and inseparable, big brother and little brother. What happened?" Johnny asked.

Dorian didn't respond.

After a few silent seconds went by, Johnny added, "Well, good news. Titus Klayton is here today."

Jordan said, *"Here? You mean here, here?* At the DMV?" He couldn't hold back his excitement.

"Yep, he's right inside. He and his brother AJ just got here. The twins are with him too."

Jordan immediately headed toward the door, fast.

"Jordan, wait a minute, son. Hold on," his father said.

"Dad, what? Uncle T and AJ are here, and, I haven't seen AJ since he was recruited to the magnet school across town. Let's go."

Dorian's slight hesitation was enough for Jordan to get through the doors of the DMV first.

As Jordan approached the Klayton family inside, Dorian watched his son hugging each of them through the glass of the front door.

Instead of walking through the door, Dorian just stood there. For a brief moment, he tried to distract himself by looking down at his phone. Eventually, he felt the group of reporters as they watched his awkward reaction.

For one of the first times in his life, former All-American, Dorian Banks felt uncertain about what to do next.

But there was something that Dorian *did know* — he knew that he wasn't mentally prepared to see Titus yet.

He looked up as he watched Titus and Jordan embracing each other inside the DMV. Jordan pointed in his father's direction from inside, as if he was answering a question from Titus that asked, *"How's your dad doing anyway, I haven't talked to him in a while?"*

"Look, he's right there," Dorian imagined his son saying.

Now that everyone saw him standing outside, Dorian knew that he couldn't retreat. He turned to look back at Cork and Johnny while they stood with the other reporters.

Johnny leaned over to Cork and asked, "Hey man, is it just me, or is something up with Dorian?"

"You know how life is. Time changes things — and time definitely changes people," Cork said. "Who knows!"

Cork turned towards Dorian as he yelled across the parking lot, "Go ahead, Dorian, go inside and see your family, it's been a while — they miss you, man."

Pastor Eddie stood at the front customer counter next to Miss Minnie. Every now and then, he often nudged her to direct her attention towards the door of the DMV as people walked in — a familiar nudge that never went unnoticed by Miss Minnie.

"It must be Christmas. Look who it is now, celebrities coming from everywhere today," Eddie whispered to Miss Minnie.

"Is that Mr. Dorian Banks?" Minnie whispered back to Eddie with a slight smile. "I am so happy to see him. His mother Weida and I were very close."

"Why's he just standing outside the door?" Eddie asked.

"If I had to guess, I'd say he's probably sending that last email or answering that last phone call before he walks into my DMV — *because he knows my rules*," Minnie said with attitude.

Dorian Banks finally found the courage to walk through the doors. Like always, he headed straight to the counter to hug Miss Minnie.

As he walked in, he looked towards Titus Klayton and the rest of his family.

Titus responded by pumping his two fists in the air, in a specific motion towards Dorian — a special greeting they established for each other during Titus's freshman year in high school.

Wow, he remembered it after all these years, Dorian thought to himself.

Not only was Titus the only freshman playing varsity that year, but he was good enough to *start as a freshman,* along with Dorian, who was the senior captain of the team and a future hall-of-famer. Their big brother / little brother relationship was instantly forged from that moment on.

After seeing Titus greet him, the awkwardness that Dorian felt walking into the DMV was immediately broken with such a familiar response from Titus.

Dorian responded back with the second part of the routine they made up years ago: two fists punching the air, followed by two quick fist-taps on his chest.

Everyone in the DMV was energized by watching the two familiar friends from Clairmont reunite with each other.

Miss Minnie glowed and beamed with pride when she saw the two interact. Eventually, Dorian arrived at the front counter.

Miss Minnie said, "Baby boy, I am so proud of you, Mr. Banks. I'll come round and hug you in a minute after I get unburied from all this paperwork."

"No worries, Miss Minnie, it's so good to see you too."

Then Dorian turned towards Eddie.

"Paster E, how you been? It's been a while!"

"Yes, it has been a while, *hasn't it,*" Pastor Eddie said in the usual *why haven't I seen you in church lately* type of way.

"Sorry you haven't seen me in a while," Dorian said, "But Lisa and I still support Calvary Baptist every way we can."

"I know that, Dorian, and it is good to see you." Eddie said. "We certainly appreciate your tithes and offerings, but it would be even better to see you in church every now and then."

"I know, Paster Eddie. Ever since we started going to Seacoast Church, the kids love it, Lisa loves it, and between that, work, and shuttling the kids around, my weekends are slammed," Dorian said.

Jordan walked over to jump into the conversation.

"He won't be shuttling ME around anymore, Pastor Eddie," Jordan added.

"Jordan, you've grown up so fast," Eddie observed.

"Pastor, I was just telling him that in the car." Dorian said, "So thanks for getting my back on that one!"

Pastor Eddie said, "You kids and these modern churches today, with your apps and live streaming, I'm sorry, but Calvary Baptist just ain't big enough for all that yet. We do miss you all being with us, but I guess as long as you're walking strong with Jesus, that's all that matters."

Minnie interrupted.

"Dorian, you know my rules. Did you take care of your business outside before you walked into my DMV," she said as she looked down at Dorian's phone.

"See, Miss Minnie, that's why I love you," Dorian said. "Some things never change. You know my mother really did love you dearly. You were the closest friend she ever had."

"Ummm humm," Minnie said. "Don't you *my momma this and my momma that* to me."

Then, Minnie pointed to Pastor Eddie.

"Eddie, go ahead and give Dorian his chance to be a part of this community again."

Dorian said, "Community? Community? I live here, what do you mean *be a part of this community again?*"

"I'm talking bout the DMV community," Minnie said.

Eddie shoved the black box in front of Dorian.

Dorian knew exactly what to do with his phone.

"Miss Minnie, I really am expecting a big call. I'm sure you've been following the news, but Boeing is helping another major airline that had its whole fleet of planes grounded by the FAA because of electrical issues. My supply chain team is buried right now trying to help them get access to the supplies they need."

Out of nowhere, Judge Frank Fox interrupted.

Judge Fox said, "Yes, buried. What a great choice of words. Sorry to interrupt, but I am buried myself and I really need to get going," as he looked at Miss Minnie.

The judge turned towards Dorian.

"By the way, fine things you're doing in the community, Mr. Dorian Banks. You're representing South Carolina extremely well," Judge Fox said.

Dorian Banks was a nice guy and a true gentleman. But he was unsure about how he should respond to Judge Fox, so his initial reaction was to immediately look over his shoulder towards Titus Klayton.

Up until this moment, Dorian didn't have a chance to make his way over to talk to Titus yet. But with Judge Fox in his face, Dorian surely didn't want to offend Titus by acting *too friendly* towards the judge. And Titus understood exactly why Dorian was looking at him — it was out of respect.

"It's all good," Titus said, as he gave Dorian a motion of approval. "Go ahead, it's okay."

Really? Dorian thought to himself.

Turning towards Judge Fox, Dorian returned the kindness.

"Great to see you too, Judge Fox. I hope your Christmas season goes well."

Miss Minnie re-interrupted.

"Frank Fox, please take a seat. We will be with you in a moment."

"Yes ma'am," Judge Fox said as he hurried off.

Minnie turned her attention back to Dorian.

"Boeing's business is Boeing's business. Do you need to step back outside to make one last call before you hand your phone to us? Better yet, you can leave it in your car while you're out there. Normally I wouldn't allow you back in. But since there is a global disruption with all these flights being grounded, I will allow you to step out to make one quick call."

Pastor Eddie was shocked. After many years of working with Miss Minnie at that DMV, he had never, *ever*, seen her allow someone to step out and make a call.

Dorian knew that he had two options and both of them were bad. The first option was the worst, though. If he did make the phone call to check in with his team at Boeing, he would be forced to back out of his promise to Jordan. He knew that the moment he made that call, his leadership team would request his presence at work, and Jordan would be disappointed that he broke his promise to stay with him for his driver's exam.

The second option wasn't good either. If he did NOT make the call to check in with his leaders, and if he left his phone in his car while he waited with Jordan in the DMV, there was a chance that he could miss the call if his teammates needed something. With a global crisis at hand, Dorian knew that it would be unprofessional to set aside his responsibility to Boeing, especially as a leader.

So, Dorian Banks did what he was trained to do in tough situations like this — *he tried to stall.*

"Miss Minnie, can you please give me a few moments?" he begged. "I'm trying to figure out what to do at work, but I don't want to disappoint Jordan because getting his drivers license is a big moment and I promised to experience it with him."

Minnie said, *"Jordan? Jordan?* You're worried about your son right now, Dorian Banks?"

Dorian looked confused when she said that.

"Well... yeah, actually I am," he answered. "Because I promised him that I'd stay for his driver's test."

Miss Minnie said, "Dorian Banks, we have a global supply chain meltdown, they need your to help fix it, and you're worried about a 16-year-old boy who's wearing two-hundred-dollar Air Jordan shoes and a jacket with a name that's so expensive I can't even pronounce it? Are you kidding me? You're worried about Jordan right now? Trust me, your son is just fine. Besides, every now and then, adults have to act like adults and YOU, Mr. Dorian Banks, need to go handle your business."

"Really? You don't think he'll be mad?" Dorian asked.

"He's a teenager," Minnie said. "Of course he'll be mad. But in a few minutes he'll be distracted by the next thing that comes along and he'll forget about it.

"Of course he'll be mad! But in a few minutes he'll be distracted by the next thing that comes along!"

Maybe I can just stay here a little longer, Dorian thought to himself.

"Miss Minnie, how long will it take for him to take his driver's test?" he asked.

She replied, "Dorian, it's two days before Christmas and this place is packed. It could be hours before Jordan takes his driving test. And, there's a snowstorm that could be headed our way."

"Snow?" Dorian confirmed. *"In South Carolina?"*

"That's right, happens about once every twenty years here," Minnie said. "Anyway, we might be forced to shut down early. Jordan might not even get a chance to take his test today at all."

Faced with a decision to make, Dorian was willing to take a gamble. He thought to himself, *Maybe I could leave for a few minutes, go check in at work, and then get back in time for Jordan's exam.*

Dorian said, "Miss Minnie, you promise to let me back in if I step out for a minute?"

Pastor Eddie leaned in to hear the answer because he had never seen Miss Minnie do this before. As a matter of fact, the whole entire DMV got quiet as they leaned in to hear the answer. Miss Minnie knew that if she allowed Dorian to leave and come back, everyone in the room would know that she broke one of her very own rules.

So, in the loudest, non-screaming voice she could come up with, she made sure that everyone in the DMV heard her response.

Minnie said, "Because there is a national emergency in the airline industry, I will permit you to re-enter my DMV today."

Pastor Eddie turned towards Dorian and he whispered under his breath, "You better get out of here before she changes her mind."

FOR *DISRUPTORS* ONLY

Many people struggle to SHOW UP *for others because they don't consistently show up for themselves. The reverse is also true. When you learn to show up for others, you will naturally become* UNSELFISH *and* MATURE. *Learning to show up for others will* BOOST YOUR CONFIDENCE *and create higher drive and motivation to achieve your own goals.*

Disruptors know that everything great begins with showing up. If you show up consistently for yourself at school, work, or even showing up to the gym to train, your life will be better. It's not very complicated. The moments when you don't FEEL LIKE *showing up are the best moments to force yourself to* DO IT ANYWAY — *you will increase your self-respect and confidence to keep moving forward.*

Scene

9

BIG BROTHER LITTLE BROTHER

 **DORIAN'S MOMENT**

When Dorian Banks prepared to leave the DMV, he realized that he needed to take a moment to officially embrace his friend and brother, Titus Klayton.

First, he had to deliver the disappointing news to his son Jordan that he needed to leave.

"Hey J-Man, can I chat with you real quick?" Dorian asked.

After sixteen years, Jordan could tell when his father had bad news for him.

"Sure, Pops, what you need?" he said.

Dorian noticed that Titus was looking in his direction.

"Hold on a moment, Jordan, I don't want to be rude — can you give me a quick minute to go over and say hello to Titus?"

"Sure dad, just grab me when you're ready," Jordan said.

As he walked over to greet Titus, Dorian was blocked once again by another emotion — the wheelchair that Titus was sitting in.

What is that all about? Dorian wondered.

Dorian hadn't seen the wheelchair up until this very moment because he assumed that Titus was sitting in a regular chair like the other customers were.

Titus was sitting alone. His little brother AJ and the twins, Gabby and Dori, were busy visiting with the Murphy twins. Once Titus was settled in with his customer ticket in hand, it didn't take long before the new lovebirds AJ and Addie were reconnected.

It was a perfect match for AJ Klayton and Addie Murphy. Addie had a twin sister, and AJ loved being "Uncle AJ" to his twin nieces. Titus was actually enjoying a few moments of time alone as the rest of the family connected. The media circus surrounding him had been pretty hectic since his return to the Charleston area.

Everyone at the DMV was surprised to see that Titus had a moment of peace to himself as he waited for his ticket to be called.

Dorian found it much harder to approach Titus knowing that a potential one-on-one conversation might happen, so he stood still for a moment as he contemplated what to say when he finally talked to Titus. While he hesitated, Mendy Donner, the local reporter, was able to reach Titus before Dorian did.

In a big way, Dorian was relieved to see Mendy step in, because he took the extra time to try to finish processing the fact that Titus Klayton, one of the greatest athletes he had ever shared the basketball court with, was now disabled.

Mendy Donner realized that she was forced to leave the circus of reporters outside earlier in the day, and she saw this as an opportunity to connect with Titus one on one, without all the cameras. She also noticed that Dorian was approaching Titus to speak to him at the same time she was.

Mendy acknowledged Dorian first.

"Well, if it isn't Dorian Banks," she said, as she stood directly beside Titus. "How in the heck have you been?"

"Hey Mendy. Great, everything is great. It's good to see you too," Dorian said.

"Were you about to talk to Titus also?" Mendy asked. "If I jumped in front of you I can always step aside to let you two talk."

"No, you're fine, go ahead. I will just wait over here."

Titus interrupted them both.

"Man, that's crazy, get over here. There's plenty of room for all of us."

Dorian slowly approached.

Titus said, "Pull up two chairs if you don't mind, Dorian. Here, Mendy, have a seat."

Facing Mendy, Titus continued, "Wow, look at you — the lady of the hour — it's so great to see you, Mendy. Your career really has taken off and you deserve it!"

Titus turned towards Dorian Banks.

"And you, sir, how in the world have you been, my brother?" Titus said, as he reached out his arm to shake Dorian's hand.

"Hey man, you know me," Dorian said, "I'm still trying to figure this new life out," as he grabbed Titus's hand to shake.

"I got ya!" Titus yelled. He used the handshake to pull Dorian closer in for a hug. "Come on, big brother, don't be shy, show your little brother some love," Titus said.

Being that close to Titus made the presence of his wheelchair even more real for Dorian.

Titus did most of the embracing, as Dorian just stood there. Then Titus turned his affections towards Mendy Donner.

"Get over here, pretty lady, you too," Titus demanded.

After the embrace, Mendy was too excited — she had to share her big news with Titus.

"Remember the project that I told you about during my last visit to see you?" she asked Titus.

"How could I forget," he said. "Your visit, your letters, the research you sent me, it would be impossible NOT to remember your *Truth In Media Project!*"

Dorian thought to himself, *Visits? Letters?* as he looked at Mendy Donner. Then Dorian said, "How exactly do you two know each so well?"

"Mendy started covering my case when she was in the high school journalism club. She was one of the first *real journalists* to take an interest in my story. Yep, this amazing human being really has been there since day one," Titus explained.

Mendy joined in. "Titus, I wouldn't have exactly called myself a *journalist* back then. I had absolutely no idea what I was doing yet."

"Correct! You did NOT know what you were doing, or what you were getting yourself into," Titus said with a smile. "But, you had two of the things that matter most, *passion and conviction* for the work you were doing."

As Titus fist-bumped Mendy, he noticed how stiff and uncomfortable Dorian was acting.

Because he was also brilliant when it came to engaging people, Titus knew exactly what to do.

Turning towards them both, Titus said, "Speaking of passion and conviction, Mendy, has anyone ever told you the real story of how Dorian Banks became so famous?"

"No, I don't think I've had the pleasure of hearing it," she answered.

Dorian stepped back in. "Titus, my brother. I only have a quick minute. I gotta get ready to leave in a minute, it's a work thing."

"Boeing, right?" Titus asked. "I heard you're in line for chairman of the board some day."

"No, not me. Way more work that I want to take on," Dorian said.

"Want to? Did you say *want to?*" Titus asked. "You mean, way more work than you *need to* take on."

Turning towards Mendy, Titus continued, "This dude doesn't *have to* do anything, Mendy. Dorian doesn't have to work another day in his life. He probably still has the first check he ever made in the NBA. That's why his last name is *Banks!*"

Turning back towards Dorian, Titus said, "You still have that first check, *don't you?*"

"As a matter of fact, I do," Dorian said with a smile.

"You see, Mendy," Titus said, "that's exactly what made Dorian Banks so famous. He is the hardest-working person I've ever met in my life. He never wanted the money or the fame. All he ever really wanted…"

Titus paused as he smiled and looked back at Dorian. "Come on, Dorian, help me finish the sentence. *All you ever really wanted…* come on, Dorian, say it with me. *All you ever really wanted…*" After Titus paused for another second, Dorian finally decided to join in.

"All you ever really wanted… *was an opportunity to be* **great.**" Titus and Dorian said together with a smile.

"All I ever truly wanted, Was An Opportunity To Be Great!"

After the brief laughter together, there was a slight pause in the conversation. In the quietness of the moment, each of them overheard Judge Frank Fox talking to Zach Gaston on the other side of the room.

"As you already know, Mendy," Dorian said, "Titus has had his share of tough times also. He didn't just wake up on the front cover of *Time* and *People Magazine*."

Placing his hands on Titus's shoulder, Dorian paused when he realized tears were beginning to form in his eyes.

He tried to start his sentence again.

"Hey man," Dorian said, before the tears forced him to stop and pause once more.

Titus leaned over as he grabbed Dorian's face.

"Look at me, brother," Titus begged.

Dorian continued to look away.

"DB, look at me. It's me, Titus, your little brother. You can say anything to me."

Unsure of exactly what was happening, Mendy Donner offered, "Hey guys, I'll step aside and give you guys some privacy."

"No," Dorian demanded. "It's okay, you need to hear this too."

As Dorian readjusted his seat, he turned to sit face to face with his little brother Titus.

"I'm sorry, little brother," Dorian said as he fought back tears. "I let you down."

"What on earth are you talking about, man?" Titus asked.

"I didn't just let you down once, I let you down twice. I should have never let them take you away, and I should have visited and wrote you more often."

Titus reached out to grab Dorian. As they both pulled each other closer, they pulled each other's heads in like they used to do on the basketball court during a tough moment.

Looking eye to eye, Titus said, **"Hey, what they did to me was NOT your fault, do you understand me?"**

"No, I should have done more to protect you," Dorian yelled.

"That's where you're wrong," Titus explained. "You are NOT a bad person, and neither were the people who sent me away. They are NOT bad people either, you understand that, right, Dorian?"

"How could you say that?" Dorian demanded.

Titus said, "Dorian, you tried your best to help me, and they made a mistake — they had the wrong guy. These things happen to people every day, Dorian."

"*These things happen? These things happen?*" Dorian cried out. "They take your life away from you, and they kill your wife and you say they just *made a mistake. What*?"

"Dorian, they didn't take my wife. Sara had cancer, she died of cancer," Titus said.

"No," Dorian said, as he cried out. "Sara had to deal with depression after the twins came, plus breast cancer, and on top of all of that, you get sent to prison for a crime that you didn't even do? She would still be alive if they hadn't taken you away Titus. They killed Sara."

Titus pushed his wheelchair as close to Dorian as he could get and they embraced even tighter. Other customers in the DMV couldn't help but witness the moment — especially Judge Fox and the rest of his legal team that sat with him.

Plus, everyone in that DMV already knew Titus's story.

As Darla DuVernay sat with her boyfriend, she listened to Titus and Dorian and she began to cry as she rubbed her pregnant stomach.

In a rude tone, her boyfriend said, "What's wrong with you now? You need to keep quiet, that is none of our business."

Jordan ran over to join his father and Titus. He had never witnessed his father being this emotional before — never.

"Dad, are you okay?" Jordan softly whispered.

Realizing that his son had joined them in the embrace, Dorian repeated in a softer voice, *"It should have been me, not you, it should have been me, not you."*

"Big brother," Titus said. "Look at me, things turned out perfect. Life is great, I'm great, the twins are great, AJ is great. God has blessed us so much, Dorian. Everything is great."

"Everything?" Dorian questioned, as he glanced down at Titus's wheelchair.

"What? This thing?" Titus asked, as he pounded the side of his wheelchair. "Don't even worry about this. I'll be walking, then running, then hooping with you on the basketball court again before you know it. We'll crush the thirty-and-over leagues and those young bucks won't be able to handle us."

"Uncle Titus," Jordan continued, "What happened anyway? Why happened to your legs?"

"Ever heard of something called meningitis?" he asked Jordan.

Jordan's face was blank.

"Nope, I didn't think so," Titus said. "It came from an infection that I got when I was away."

"This happened to you because you were in jail, Uncle T, in jail for something you didn't even do?" Jordan asked.

"Hey Jordan, listen," Titus explained. "A lot of good things happened to me when I was in there too. This wheelchair is just one of the bad things that happened. But don't worry, I'll beat this just like I beat everything else."

Titus grabbed the back of Dorians neck even tighter.

"You want to know *why* I'm going to beat this, Dorian?" Titus said. "Because all I need in life is — *what?* What's the only thing I need, Dorian?"

As Dorian finished wiping the tears away, he tried to hold back his smile, but he couldn't resist Titus's silly grin.

"I'm going to beat this, because all we need is what?" The three of them all joined in as they yelled out loud, *"All we need… is an opportunity to be great."*

As they finished, Titus said, "Dorian, I can't believe you've been carrying this guilt with you all these years. Dorian you *did* visit enough, you *did* write enough. I might not even be a free man today if it weren't for you."

Dorian said, "I just wish I could have done more."

"No, you did your part, Dorian, and I had to do what I had to do. That's what life is all about. And now, it's my turn to help someone else. I've got to use my fame and my platform to help others, or none of this will be worth anything."

Dorian said, "You deserve everything good that's coming your way, Titus, everything."

Jordan joined in, "Hey Uncle T, is it true that you signed a movie and a book deal worth over thirty million dollars?"

"Jordan Banks," his father yelled. "Not cool, son, not cool. That's private information. Your mother and I taught you how important privacy is when you live your life in front of the cameras."

Titus stepped in. "No, it's okay, Dorian, he's family."

Giving his full attention to Jordan, Titus said, "Everything I do is under the FR33DOM Brand now. The movie deals, book deals, car dealerships, all of it. The first part of my life was a little rough, but that's nothing compared to what Jesus went through — just for us. So I promised God that I would use the rest of my life to serve others, and that's what I'm going to do."

"That's awesome," Jordan said. "But speaking of serving others. I just turned 16, I'm getting my drivers license today, and I have a big date tonight."

"Big date? With who?" Titus questioned.

"Her name is Sophie, and I think she could be the one, Uncle Titus, for real!"

Titus said, "The one? The one what?" As everyone laughed.

"You know what I mean, the one," Jordan said. "Anyway, I might have to let Sophie know that I personally talked to Titus Klayton today, since you're a big celebrity now."

"Whatever," Titus said, "Just slow down on that *she might be the one* talk."

Mendy Donner, the news reporter, jumped back in to the conversation as she tried to control her own tears.

"I'm sorry," she said. "But this is probably the most incredible thing I've ever heard in my life. Titus, your life is such an inspiration to so many people."

Titus grabbed Mendy's hand as she wiped tears from her face.

"Hey you," Titus said. "You better get all your tears out now, because we have some serious work to do. Your *Truth In Media Project* is going to change the world, and I'm going to do everything in my power to make sure that Paramount doesn't mess this deal up."

Mendy was shocked.

"You know about Paramount?" she asked.

"*Know about it, know about it.* Are you kidding me? Do you think your agent just happened to call you out of nowhere this morning? I had to do something to help you with your project or you would have sent me 400 more emails!"

Mendy was amazed and grateful.

"Titus, I don't know what to say, this is amazing, I mean, you're amazing," she said.

"I know what you better say," Titus said. "You better say the right thing to Miss Minnie, because if you don't get your driver's license renewed today, you won't be able to flight to that Paramount meeting."

"Yes, right. Can you help me with that too?" she said.

"What? *Help you with Miss Minnie?*" Titus asked.

"Yes. Can you put in a good word to see if she'll move me to the front of the line? If this snowstorm comes today, I won't get up there at all."

"What? Cross paths with Miss Minnie on a day like this?" Titus said. "And risk the chance of losing *my spot in line* and getting kicked out? Mendy Donner, you must be crazy."

As the group all laughed together, they finished wiping what was left of their tears. The slight pause in conversation was enough for Dorian Banks to remember that he needed to leave and get back to his emergency at work.

Dorian said, "Hey Jordan."

Then Jordan interrupted him.

"Yeah, yeah, yeah, Dad. Let me guess, you need to leave to go to work, *right?*"

Dorian hesitated. "Well, it's just that…"

"I know, Pops, you have responsibilities at work also, I get it," Jordan said.

"You sure you're not upset?" Dorian asked.

"No I'm good," Jordan said, as he looked off in the opposite direction.

Dorian looked back at Titus Klayton.

"Hey TK, you mind keeping Jordan company when I split?"

"I got him. Go take care of business," Titus said. "Plus, he needs to hear some real stories about who his dad was back in the day."

"Chill out. He ain't ready for all that yet," Dorian said.

Glancing back at Jordan, Titus said, "I don't know, Dorian, something tells me that your son is ready to hear some truth while you're gone."

"Well, at least go easy on him," Dorian said, as he hugged Jordan and Titus.

Mendy yelled, "Great seeing you, Dorian Banks!"

Dorian turned back to respond. "Good luck with your Paramount tomorrow, if you actually make it there."

Turning back towards the front desk where Eddie and Miss Minnie were standing, Dorian added, "Hey, Miss Minnie, please take it easy on Mendy — she has a big day tomorrow."

"You get out of here and go get those planes back in the sky," Minnie yelled back, as if Dorian had all the power to make it happen on his own.

FOR *DISRUPTORS* ONLY

Don't avoid doing hard things.

Don't avoid having hard conversations.

Great OPPORTUNITIES come from doing hard things.

Do you EXPECT OPPORTUNITY to find you?

Do you want things HANDED TO YOU?

Do you COMPLAIN when you don't get what you want?

Attitude always reveals true character. Disruptors SEE THE POSITIVE in all things, even when they don't get what they want. If the only thing you look for is the OPPORTUNITY TO BE GREAT, you will always disrupt yourself and continue to grow.

Scene

10

"988"

Back on the airplane, as Emmett and Avery arrived to this moment in the story, they were no longer concerned about *where the story came from*. They also didn't care about the reasons why Emmett's mother, Claire Cooper, emailed the story to him. They only thing they cared about at this point *was the story*.

"Why am I crying right now?" Avery asked, as she grabbed a portion of her shirt to wipe her face.

"Because that's just what you do," Emmett responded.

"Wait, look at me, Mr. Emmett Cooper. Do I see tears in your eyes?" she said.

"What? Get out of here," he responded.

"I know exactly what it was," Avery said. "The future movie producer inside of you just couldn't take it any longer. That scene with Titus and Dorian reuniting was too much for you, wasn't it?"

Emmett rolled his eyes.

"Okay seriously though," he said. "This story is shaping up to be a movie director's dream. It has great dialogue, powerful moments, complicated characters, it's all there."

"Don't forget drama and conflict. I guess you finally got a small taste of what you wanted," Avery observed.

"Yeah, now I'm invested," Emmett said. "By the way, I noticed that the story's been called MINNIE MOMENTS the entire time, but the last scene was called DORIAN'S MOMENT, and the next scene is called JORDAN'S MOMENT."

"And…" Avery said. "You tell me, Mr. Film Director. Why'd they change the titles?"

"Only one reason why," Emmett said. "To force the audience to get ready for the plot change that's about to happen."

~~~~~~~~~~

THE TIPPING POINT

The moment Dorian Banks walked out of the DMV, his son Jordan jumped out of his seat and went straight to the bathroom. As he hurried, he accidentally kicked the bag of another customer.

"Hey, excuse you," the man said.

"What?" Jordan replied in an angry tone.

"Son, you kicked my bag and you almost stepped on my foot," the man said.

"No I didn't," Jordan responded.

The brief drama drew the attention of others in the DMV. From across the room, Titus Klayton spoke up to get Jordan's attention.

"Hey, Jordan," Titus said, as he dipped his chin to his chest, giving Jordan a look that said *you were raised better than that, so act like it, and apologize.*

Jordan understood Titus's body language loud and clear.

"Sorry if I kicked your bag, man," Jordan said.

"That's *Sir*. Sorry I kicked your bag, *Sir*," the man said as he corrected Jordan.

"Right... *Sir*."

"It's Jordan, right?" the man said.

"Huh?" Jordan responded.

"Your name. Titus Klayton just called you Jordan. That's your name, right?" the man confirmed.

"Yeah, it's Jordan. How you know Titus anyway?" Jordan replied.

The man said, "Who doesn't know Titus Klayton? His story is famous around the world and back. By the way, I'm Joe, Joe Moscufo," as he reached out to shake Jordan's hand. "And don't worry about my bag, these things happen. Just don't let it happen a second time, or you might end up taking a swim," Joe said with a sneaky smile.

"A swim?" Jordan asked with a confused look. It took a second for it to hit him. "Ohhhh, the Italian mafia thing," Jordan said, "I get it... *a swim with cement shoes*."

"Now you're getting it kid, there you go," Joe said, as he looked around the room and smiled.

In a room full of southern folks, a few of them got it, while others were still trying to figure out where the old mans accent came from.

He gave Jordan a quick head nod of approval, then Jordan was off to the bathroom.

Titus wasn't sure, but a small part of him thought that something was going on with Jordan. *Is he mad that Dorian left?* he thought to himself. As always, Titus trusted his gut instinct.

He motioned for his younger brother AJ to come over.

"Hey, what's up with Jordan?" Titus asked AJ.

AJ said, "Addie and I were just talking about that. But I wouldn't know. I haven't seen Jordan much since I transferred schools, but Addie and Callie said that he gets like that sometimes."

"He get's like what?" Titus asked.

"You know, all anxious and stuff."

"Anxious? What do you mean anxious?" Titus clarified.

"Like I said, I'm not too sure," AJ added, "But I know he used to flip out about his parents a lot when we were younger."

"Flip out? Parents?" Titus questioned.

"You know what I mean," AJ assumed. "Some C-Kids just don't adjust well to normal life."

"C-Kids? What do you mean?" Titus stopped himself before he continued. "Ohhhh, okay, you mean Celebrities-Kids."

"Yep," Jordan confirmed.

"Does his father Dorian know that Jordan has been having a hard time?" Titus asked.

"Like I said, big bro, I don't really see Jordan much anymore. Addie and Callie see him every day at school though."

Titus said, "Okay, that makes sense. Hey, tell the twins to come over here for a minute."

"Which twins?" AJ clarified.

Smiling, Titus said, "Yeah, good point. Addie and Callie."

After motioning for them to join the conversation, Titus's twin girls Gabby and Dori came also.

Titus said, "Jordan, can you take your nieces back over there to color with them for a minute while I speak to Addie and Callie?"

"Sure," Jordan said as he guided the little ones away.

After greeting the twins, Titus said, "Hey Addie, you keeping my little brother straight?"

"I'm trying my best Mr. Titus." she said.

"Addie, please, call me Titus."

Turning towards Callie, Titus said, "What about you? How you doing? Hopefully my brother and your sister aren't annoying you too much with their puppy love. I know stuff like that can drive a twin crazy!"

Callie said, "Sometimes they do. Okay, well, most of the time they do, but they're awesome together. They sure will make a great team as attorneys one day!"

"Yes they will," Titus agreed.

Readdressing them both, Titus asked, "So what's up with Jordan? He looked pretty upset as he stormed off. You see him like that much?"

The twins turned towards each other at the same time, unsure of what to say.

Titus said, "AJ told me that Jordan gets anxious a lot. What's that about?"

The twins were still reluctant to respond.

"Girls. Just let me ask you this, *is it anything serious?* If not, you can plead the 5th. You don't have to snitch on anyone if it's not serious."

Titus was basically an expert when it came to non-verbal cues and body language. Spending time in prison forced him to develop instincts to recognize everything — nothing got past him Titus anymore. When he noticed Callie shift in her seat and look down to the left out of the corner of her eyes, he knew something was going on.

"Callie, what is it?" Titus questioned.

She immediately looked back at Addie.

"I can't," Callie said. "Addie you tell him."

Titus tried to respect the fact that they had something to share as he patiently waited for an answer. But after another period of silence, his instincts still told him that something bigger was going on with Jordan.

He became more direct.

"Addie, please," Titus said in a louder tone.

Other people in the DMV looked over at them when Titus raised his voice, so he dropped his head and talked softer to deflect some of the attention.

Addie leaned in closer to Titus.

"Okay, here's what happened," she said, after pausing to take a deep breath. "So Callie and Jordan used to date, well, kind of date. But it never really went too far because Jordan started acting really weird, right away."

"Weird? What do you mean *weird?*" Titus asked.

"You know, acting all clingy and stuff. Texting a million times a day and all hours through the night. Then he saw Callie talking to her friend Robert at school one day and he lost it — got all jealous and stuff — even though he and Callie had only been talking for a few days."

"So, he's a guy. He was excited about a new girl, and he wanted to talk and text a lot. Then he got jealous about another guy, what's wrong with that?" Titus asked.

"That's not it," Addie explained. "After only a few days of dating, when Callie told him she just wanted to be friends, he lost it."

"What do you mean, he lost it?" Titus questioned.

"I don't know if I can say the words out loud," Addie said.

Callie leaned in abruptly.

"He threatened to kill himself," she said.

Titus yelled out, "What? Jordan?"

He realized he needed to lower his voice again.

"Kill himself? Jordan Banks, you sure he said that?"

Callie leaned over to show Titus the screenshots of the texts that Jordan sent.

"What are these?" he asked.

"Screenshots." Callie said.

"Screenshots, for real?" he confirmed.

Titus instantly grabbed the phone from Callie.

"What are you doing with that phone in here?" Titus said. "If Miss Minnie sees you with this she's gonna kick us all out of here."

"No, Mr. Titus, I'm sorry, I mean *Titus*. You need to see this," Callie explained.

After looking down at the phone, what Titus saw was undeniable. When he finished scrolling through the text messages, he looked up and said, "Jordan Banks? Jordan sent you this?"

"Yes," Callie confirmed.

After seeing the screenshots, Titus was speechless for a moment. It didn't feel real. He thought to himself, *What? Dorian and Jillian's son?*

Addie placed her hand on top of Titus's hand, as if she knew exactly what Titus was thinking.

"Yes, Titus, your big brother Dorian's son. I know it's probably crazy to hear all of this."

After placing his head down in his lap, Titus had no idea what to do next. He'd seen other people face plenty of depression and suicide situations when he was away, but this was different. He was too close to Dorian.

"When did this happen?" he asked.

"Last month," Callie responded.

"Did you show this to anyone?" he asked.

"No," both of the twins answered together.

Callie said, "Jordan made me swear not to say anything and I didn't want to embarrass him or make things worse. I was just afraid he would hurt himself."

Titus knew how bad that type of guilt could impact the emotions of someone, *especially a teenager,* so he leaned over and hugged Callie.

"Callie, babygirl. I'm so sorry this happened to you. How have you been doing, are you okay?"

"To be honest, not good. But at least I have my sister."

The two twins embraced.

"She didn't want to tell me at first," Addie offered. "But twins always know when something's going on with the other one, always. Callie was acting all weird and I knew it had something to do with Jordan, so I forced her to tell me."

Titus instantly looked towards the corner of the room where his little brother AJ and his twins were playing.

"That's for sure. Twins really are something special," Titus agreed.

Addie leaned closer to Titus.

She said, "After Callie told me what happened, I made her dial 988."

"988? What is that," Titus asked.

"It's brand new, it just came out. It's like calling 911, but it's for mental health and suicide type of situations."

"988 huh? Okay, that's good," Titus said. "What did they say when you called?"

Callie spoke up. "I didn't really tell them anything. I didn't even tell them Jordan's name."

"Hey, it's cool, you're okay Callie. Don't worry about it. Just tell me what they said." Titus said.

"The counselor on the phone just helped me out because she knew that I was upset. They wanted me to do more, but I didn't want to call the police or anything."

Addie stepped back in, "There was no way I was going to be the only other person who knew about it. That was way too much pressure for me."

Titus asked, "Have you talked to Jordan lately? Is he okay?"

Callie said, "Thankfully it seems like he moved on."

"Moved on?" Titus said. He looked confused.

"He's crushing on a new girl now, Sophie."

"I guess he moved on fast," Titus said.

Addie said, "The problem with that is, we heard she didn't really like Jordan. She was interested in him at first because his dad was famous and everything, but then Jordan started acting all weird with her too, just like he did with Callie.

Then Callie added, "It's too bad. Now they say Sophie's been talking to another guy named Chase."

Addie jumped back in, "Yep, and Sophie just updated her relationship status online a few minutes ago."

"What do you mean *she changed her status?*" Titus asked.

"Now it says she's *in a Relationship With Chase Mortenson*," Addie said.

"You think that's why Jordan's so upset?" Titus asked.

Callie said, "No, and I'm afraid what might happen when he does find out. I snuck my phone into the DMV, that's how I found out. But Jordan doesn't know yet."

Then Addie said, "Jordan's in the bathroom and he's mad right now, probably because his dad left. He's always complaining that his parents don't really love him, they never spend any time with him, stuff like that."

Titus couldn't move. On the outside his body was frozen. On the inside, he trembled like an earthquake because he already knew he had to share this information with Dorian — the same Dorian Banks who had the most mental strength and resiliency of anyone that Titus had ever met. Sharing this info with him about his son wasn't going to be easy.

Dorian's son? Titus thought to himself. *Struggling with anxiety and depression... threatening suicide... Dorian Banks' son?*

Titus's heart was also breaking for Jordan. He also knew that Jordan was planning his big date with Sophie. Knowing that Jordan had previously threatened to hurt himself, forced Titus to take action. *I have to do something*, he thought to himself. *But what?*

FOR *DISRUPTORS* ONLY

Sometimes we never truly know what a person is going through. Titus was shocked to hear that Jordan's life was potentially in danger. Every time we hear that something bad has happened to a someone that we care about, it captures our immediate attention.

Disruptors learn to MAKE A DIFFERENCE for others with random calls, texts or visits when no one is expecting it. If someone is on your mind and you don't know why, take the time to reach out to them.

Disruptors have the CONFIDENCE and COMPASSION to show others that they care about them. If you want to live a greater life, try to find ways each day, to positively CONTRIBUTE to others around you.

11

JORDAN'S MOMENT

 **JORDAN'S MOMENT**

When Jordan finally stepped out of the bathroom, the first person he made eye contact with was Judge Frank Fox. Jordan didn't know Judge Fox well, but he knew that he was the judge that sent his Uncle Titus to jail.

When Titus noticed the scowl on Jordan's face, he turned around to see who Jordan was looking at.

Titus Klayton and Judge Fox had managed to avoid eye contact up until that moment.

Titus turned to look back at Jordan.

"Hey, hey you, look at me," he said to Jordan.

"Yeah, Uncle T?"

"Don't do that. That type of anger won't ever get you anywhere in life," Titus said.

"What? I just looked at him," Jordan said. "Why are you so cool about things with Judge Fox anyway?"

Titus said, "Because I have a bigger purpose in this world, Jordan, and so do you."

"What does purpose have to do with what Judge Fox did to you? I mean, he took most of your life away," Jordan said.

As Jordan got closer, Titus reached into his bag to pull a book out.

Jordan noticed the front cover.

"Uncle T, is that you? Is that your new book?"

"Yep," Titus confirmed. "It's not even out yet, but this copy is for you."

"Nice title, Uncle T," Jordan said, as he read the book title louder than usual: "*FR33DOM: 33 Reasons to Love, Live & Forgive.*"

Several people in the DMV focused on Jordan as he read the title out loud. Others couldn't help themselves from turning to stare directly at Judge Fox.

Titus grabbed a Sharpie pen out of his bag to endorse the book. As he signed it, he couldn't stop thinking about the conversation he just had with the Murphy Twins about Jordan's mental health.

Titus knew exactly what to write in the book.

> JORDAN:
>
> Always choose life.
> Keep God first.
> Learn to love and forgive yourself.
> Learn to love forgive and forgive others.
> ~ Uncle T.

Jordan looked down at the inscription in the book. He immediately looked back up at Addie and Callie, who were still sitting next to Titus.

Although Jordan swore Callie to secrecy about his "bad day that he had" — *which is what Jordan brushed it off as* — he could tell by the look on their faces that something was up.

"Jordan, have a seat," Titus said.

"Why? What's going on?"

"Jordan, just have a seat so I can talk to you for a moment," Titus said.

"Why? What did they say to you?" Jordan asked, as he looked at Addie and Callie. "Whatever they said isn't true. It isn't true, Uncle T. I'm good, I'm good, alright?"

"You sure you're alright?"

"Yeah, I'm sure."

"If you're alright, then you shouldn't have a problem sitting down. Now take a seat, Jordan," Titus demanded.

Feeling embarrassed, Jordan looked around the room before he sat down. Then he chose the seat next to Addie, sitting as far away from Callie as possible.

Titus Klayton was an educated, smart and extremely sharp individual — *he didn't miss anything*. He also had a series of life experiences that sharpened his awareness even more. If there was one thing he'd learned, especially after spending many years of his life dealing with other inmates in prison, he'd learned that no two situations were the same, and every new situation required a new, unique approach. But if something was serious enough, he also knew that the best way to handle it was by being direct.

"Jordan, you told me you were good, right?" Titus said.

"For sure," Jordan responded.

"Okay then. So you're telling me that your parents don't need to be worried about you?" Titus asked.

"Why, what do you care?" Jordan responded.

"What do I care? Boy, do you know who you're talking to? Listen, Jordan, I have never seen you act this way. What's going on with you, boy? Be real with me — do we need to be worried about you, Jordan?"

"They don't care anyway," Jordan said.

"Who doesn't care? Of course I care about you, Jordan."

"Yeah, I know *you* care," Jordan said. "Now my dad, on the other hand, all he ever cared about was work."

After hearing Jordan's words, Titus glanced over at Addie. Jordan's words basically confirmed that Addie was right. Jordan *was angry* with his parents.

"Jordan, you have no idea how much your father loves you, do you?" Titus said. "I was there the day you were born and I have never seen your father happier."

"Well, you want to know something?" Jordan said. "I once read that the average father in America spends less than eight minutes of actual face time with his kids everyday. Eight minutes — that's it! And you know what? Dorian Banks spends less time than that with his kids. So what do you have to say about that, Uncle T. Since you want to sit here and tell me how much my father loves me."

Titus hesitated for a moment to gather his thoughts.

Jordan continued, "And another thing, no disrespect or anything, but Uncle T, you've been gone for a long time, and people change. Maybe you don't know my father as well as you think you do."

Titus said, "See now, that is where you're wrong, Jordan. Because I once felt the same way about your father as you do right now. Don't forget, he was my big brother and my best friend, and I wanted to hang out with him every day and every minute, just like you want to. Sometimes I felt like your dad just ghosted me, and left me alone. He would disappear all the time."

Now Titus Klayton had Jordan's attention.

"He did?" Jordan asked. "What happened?"

"What happened?" Titus said with a smile. "What happened is right there in my new book that you're holding. Go ahead and open it up."

Jordan opened the book.

"Turn to page 36," Titus said.

Jordan thought that was odd.

"Page 36, why that page? That's really specific."

"Just open up the book and you'll see," Titus said.

Jordan opened to page 36 and began to read.

If I chose to be angry about the things that were taken out of my life, I would have missed out on seeing all of the blessings that I did have in my life. Although I felt abused and let down from other leaders around me, I still knew what was expected of me as a leader. I knew that I was called to be a leader because I was taught by one of the greatest leaders the world has ever seen ~ Dorian Banks.

After reading that part, Jordan stopped to look up at Titus.

Titus said, "No, you're not done yet, keep reading."

As our captain and team leader, we wanted Dorian around all of the time. There were times when my teammates and I wanted to hang out, especially with Dorian because he was always so much fun. But instead of hanging out with us, he always complained about saving his money and not wasting it going out.

Most of the time, if we weren't at basketball practice or in school, Dorian was nowhere to be found — we couldn't find him anywhere, I mean anywhere. After we'd had enough of his excuses about not wasting his money, or not hanging out with us, my teammates and I started following Dorian after basketball practice. It didn't take long before we realized how Dorian was spending all of his money and why he didn't have the time to hang out with us goofing off.

From that moment on, if we ever needed to find Dorian Banks, we knew we could find him at one of the 3 H's — the hospital, hospice home or the homeless shelter — that's where Dorian Banks donated most of his time. He used any leftover money that he did have to buy food or supplies for people who didn't have anything. That's who Dorian Banks was, and that's what a true leader is.

Jordan didn't know what to think. First, he sat for a moment as he looked at Titus.

But Jordan was still bitter.

He said to Titus, "Okay I get it. He used to do a bunch of nice stuff for people, but I'm his son, what about me?"

Titus said, "Jordan, you're right. People do change. But let me tell you something: *it's really tough for a person to change who they are at the core of their heart.*"

> " *It's tough for a person to change who they are at the core of their heart.* "

"Ain't I supposed to be in the core of his heart?" Jordan asked. "Why can't he spend more time with me?"

Titus said, "Jordan, does your father get home late at night from work?"

Jordan said, "Yes. He always has."

"Also, when you and your mom traveled with your father to away games when you were young, did he ever disappear after the press conferences and leave you and your mother in your hotel room waiting for him?"

"Yep. That's exactly what happened, 99% of the time," Jordan said.

"Where do you think he was after those games, Jordan?" Titus said. "And where do you think he is early in the morning or in the evening when he isn't at work or at home?"

"I don't know," Jordan replied.

Titus said, "Jordan, do you even know where the local homeless shelter is son?"

Jordan looked puzzled.

"Jordan, you're not a man yet," Titus said, "but you will be soon, so it's time you understand something about life. Your life is a secret, a secret that nobody knows except God. And for the rest of your life, Jordan, **your job is to take one step closer, every day, so God can reveal more and more of that secret to you, because that secret is connected to your purpose in this world.**"

Addie and Callie both slid down in their seats a little bit.

Addie leaned over to whisper in Callie's ear, "He's being a bit tough on him, don't ya think?"

Titus intercepted her words, "No, no, I'm not at all Addie," he said loudly, drawing the attention of Miss Minnie and Pastor Eddie. "This young man sitting in front of me has a decision to make."

"I do? What decision is that?" Jordan asked.

"Leaders must take responsibility for their lives, Jordan," Titus said. "That's the biggest part of what it means to choose life. Leaders who choose life know that they're responsible for the choices and decisions they make, regardless of what happens around them or how someone else makes them feel. Jordan, your father was forced to grow up faster than most kids after your grandparents died, he was forced to figure out who he was earlier than most people. That's why your dad has more self-awareness and emotional intelligence that anyone else you'll ever meet. That's why Dorian Banks lives with purpose every day, son. Do you understand what I'm trying to say to you, Jordan? Jordan, you've had everything given to you, so you won't understand the man that your father is until you become a man yourself."

Jordan said, "Okay, Okay, I hear you. But why do you keep saying that I have to choose life? Geez, Uncle T, what did Addie and Callie say to you anyway?"

Titus said, "Jordan, stop asking me that, and stop playing games with me. You know exactly what they said to me. Life isn't just about you, Jordan, your actions have consequences. Did you ever think about what you put Callie though by threatening to hurt yourself?"

As soon as Titus said that, Miss Minnie interrupted.

"Hurt himself? Hurt himself? Is everything okay over here? Anything I need to know about?"

"I'm not sure yet, Miss Minnie, I'm waiting for Jordan to answer that for himself," Titus said.

"Man, get off my back, I said I'm alright," Jordan yelled. "You know I wouldn't ever do anything to hurt myself. I was just saying that, now can you just drop it?"

"Look at me, Jordan! You have a great life, a fantastic life! God has blessed your family with wealth, health and love for each other. But at some point you're going to have to grow up and stop acting like a spoiled and entitled brat!"

"Entitled? Spoiled? Why you say that?" Jordan asked.

"Because I've seen everything there is to see in this world, Jordan — the good and the bad," Titus said. "And trust me, the only people who threaten to hurt themselves are people who either just want attention, or they're just mad that they didn't get what they wanted, or, sometimes when people threaten to hurt themselves, they really do need medical attention to help them get their lives back on track."

"I'm not spoiled. And I'm not entitled," Jordan said.

"Do you need medical attention? Do you think you need a doctor to help you figure this out?" Titus said. "Because if you do we can make that happen?"

Embarrassed once again, Jordan looked around the DMV as everyone tuned in to the scene.

Miss Minnie joined in, "*Titus Klayton,* maybe this isn't the best place or time for this."

"No, Miss Minnie, I have all the respect in the world for you, but I have to disagree. Like I said, I've seen what happens in this world and how lives are affected when one person makes a bad choice or decision."

Judge Fox and Zach Gaston both looked at each other when Titus said that.

Darla DuVernay held her pregnant stomach tighter as she sharply looked at her boyfriend.

Mendy Donner wanted to do something to help Jordan, but she felt like whatever she said would just make things worse.

Then, Pastor Eddie stepped in.

He said, "Titus, Jordan, if you don't mind, is it okay if I take a moment to pray for you right now?"

Titus said, "Sure, maybe in a minute Pastor E, but I'm not done with Jordan yet."

He turned his attention back to Jordan.

"Jordan, if you don't have a medical condition, what is it then? Are you just trying to get attention?"

"No, of course not. I mean, I don't know," Jordan said. "Just leave me alone. I said I'm okay."

Titus said, "Oh, so that's it? You threatened to hurt yourself because you didn't get something you wanted. Let me ask you this, are you gonna go round your whole life acting immature and spoiled every time you don't get what you want? Will you ever learn to deal with disappointment like a healthy human being?"

Jordan looked rejected and everyone could feel it too.

In that exact moment, a small part inside of Titus's heart felt a slight shift. Titus thought that maybe Addie, Callie and Miss Minnie were right, maybe this wasn't the time or the place.

Should I go easier on him? Titus thought to himself.

"No, I can't afford to," Titus whispered out loud.

"Can't afford to what?" Miss Minnie asked.

"Never mind, Miss Minnie," he said.

Titus knew the consequences. He fully understood what could happen if a person didn't make healthy choices, and he also knew that 42% of deaths by suicide with teens and young adults were caused by relationship issues. The bottom line was, he knew that there were some choices that a person could never come back from — *like suicide*. **Titus knew to take it seriously when a person threatened to take their own life**.

He leaned over to Callie.

"Give me the phone," Titus said.

"Why?" she asked.

"Just give me the phone, please?" he demanded.

Miss Minnie was steaming mad. "Now hold on a minute..."

Titus interrupted Miss Minnie as he used his arm to push her away.

"Miss Minnie, relax," Titus said, as he made strong eye contact with Jordan Banks. "This could be a life-or-death situation that we're dealing with, so just let me handle this."

Callie handed Titus the phone.

"Unlock it and pull up the screenshots," Titus demanded.

Jordan stood up quickly.

"What are you doing? He asked. "I said to just leave me alone. Why are you doing this to me, Uncle T?"

Titus held the screenshots in Jordan's face.

"Is this you? Did you write these messages to Callie, or did someone else send them?" Titus said.

"Yes, I sent them, why?" Jordan asked.

"Don't ask me why!" Titus yelled. "You need to tell me why. Why did you threaten to take your own life?"

"I don't know!" Jordan screamed out loud.

"Was it because of a girl, because someone broke up with you?"

"I said I don't know. I don't know why I sent them."

"Okay then," Titus said. "What about Sophie?"

"What about Sophie?" Jordan asked.

Addie and Callie were shocked.

"Please don't say anything Titus," Addie begged.

"Say anything about what?" Jordan demanded.

Titus said, "So, is Sophie your next obsession Jordan, you stalking her now too?"

"What are you talking about? I never stalked anyone." Jordan said.

"Ohhh, okay. What about the date that you're supposed to have with Sophie tonight?"

"What about it?" Jordan said.

Titus looked back at Callie as he handed the phone back to her.

She took her phone back and Titus said, "No, hold on, Callie. I still need your phone, I'm not done with it. Open up that app for me please."

"What app?" Callie asked.

"You know which app, just open it up!" Titus screamed.

Miss Minnie couldn't stand back any longer.

She said, "This is exactly why I don't allow phones in my building — they ain't nothing but trouble."

Turning towards Pastor Eddie, Minnie said, "Eddie, please get that black box right now."

Eddie didn't move. He looked at Titus for confirmation.

"Eddie, did you hear me?" Minnie yelled.

Titus said, "Don't move, Pastor, I said I've got this," as he reached to grab the phone away from Callie once more.

Titus looked down at the phone to confirm that it was opened to Sophie's online profile.

The moment was tense and no one in the DMV moved an inch as they all waited to see what Titus was going to do next.

In what seemed to be the slowest motion ever experienced in a live moment, Titus wheeled his chair closer to Jordan and he flipped the phone around in Jordan's face.

"Is Sophie still going out with you tonight?" Titus asked.

As Jordan looked down at the phone, he saw her updated relationship status for the first time.

Even though he didn't realize it, Jordan started to read Sophie's status update out loud.

"*In A Relationship With Chase Mortenson...*" Jordan said.

As soon as he read it, a switch flipped inside of him.

"WHAT... IS... THIS?" Jordan screamed out loud.

There it was, the moment that Titus Klayton was waiting for.

If there was any doubt about Jordan's inability to be resilient in the face of challenges, especially when he didn't get what he wanted, this moment revealed everything.

"I knew it, I knew it," Jordan screamed. "Nobody cares about me! I might as well kill myself right now!"

And there it was, the moment Titus Klayton was waiting for. The moment Titus knew had to occur if Jordan would ever have a chance to be honest with himself.

Jordan took off running and Titus unsuccessfully tried to reach out to grab him, as Jordan shocked and scared everyone in the DMV when he screamed, *"Nobody cares about me, nobody cares about me."* He ran into the bathroom to lock himself inside.

FOR *DISRUPTORS* ONLY

Although this scene may be hard for you to read, remember, uncomfortable moments force us to tune in to the needs of others. Stress and anxiety from relationship breakups are one of the leading reasons for suicide attempts among teens and young adults.

Here is a question that you should ask those who are closest to you: WHAT IS SOMETHING THAT I NEED TO HEAR, THAT COULD POTENTIALLY MAKE ME BETTER? Asking that question can potentially reveal opportunities for growth that you may have been blind to.

You should only ask this question to a person who has the self-awareness, empathy and compassion to give you a healthy response, or else, they could end up PROJECTING their own fears and negativity onto you.

Scene

12

YOGA PANTS

Emmett Cooper and his girlfriend Avery both sat motionless on the airplane. They needed to take a pause from reading the story. As they sat in silence, it was the first time that either of them had a chance to notice that the plane finally took off.

"What, we're in the air?" Emmett observed.

"I had no idea," Avery said. "I could have been in the middle of a war zone reading that story, and I wouldn't have heard a thing."

Emmett's demeanor seemed softer than usual.

"Hey, what ya thinking?" Avery asked.

"I don't know. I guess I'm conflicted a bit, especially if this is a true story. I'm not sure that Titus Klayton needed to push Jordan that hard."

"I know, right?" Avery said, "I mean, the Murphy Twins already gave him a heads up that Jordan wasn't himself lately."

"Maybe he was," Emmett said.

"Was what?" Avery clarified.

"Himself. Maybe he was himself. What if that's just who he is?" Emmett said.

"What? Suicidal?" Avery confirmed.

"No. Broken. Just broken," Emmett said.

"Are you sure you're okay reading this?" Avery asked.

"Yes, I'm good. But I can definitely see a lot of myself in this Jordan Banks character."

"How so? You aren't entitled or spoiled!" Avery said.

"Yes, but I also don't really know *who I am* either," Emmett said. "I feel like I've been in that bathroom before, or even worse, I could end up there at any time."

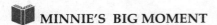 MINNIE'S BIG MOMENT

Miss Minnie ran over to the bathroom door. She wanted to demand that Jordan to come out of the bathroom, but she was smart enough to know that wouldn't be the best idea.

"Eddie, grab the keys for me please!" Minnie yelled.

"Ain't gonna do no good, the keys don't work," he said.

"What do you mean, *the keys don't work?*"

Eddie said, "The state was supposed to send someone out to fix it the last time this happened, they never came though."

Darla DuVernay's boyfriend said, *"The last time this happened? How often y'all get people wanting to kill themselves in the bathroom round around here!"*

The old Italian man, Joe Moscufo yelled out, "Hey wise guy, you shut your mouth or get out of here. Now's not the time for all that."

Realizing he was now somewhat involved in the moment, Joe Moscufo continued, "God knows this ain't none of my business. I just moved down here from up North. And honestly, there was a day when I would've laughed at a kid stuck in a bathroom like this. But we just lost a nephew who took his own life, and I had dinner with the kid the night before he did it — I still can't forgive myself."

Mendy Donner walked over to give him a hug.

"I'm sorry to hear that, sir. We're glad to have you here with us in South Carolina," she said.

Joe Moscufo said, "And I'm glad to be here, thank you, Ms. Donner. Nice program you do in the evenings by the way, my wife Carol really likes it too."

Turning back to the group, Joe Moscufo continued, "But hey everybody, we got to get the kid out of the bathroom before he hurts himself."

Standing outside of the door, Miss Minnie decided to talk her way through the situation.

"Jordan. Jordan can you hear me?" she said.

"Leave me alone, back off!" he screamed.

"Jordan, please don't do anything to hurt yourself, please, Jordan," Minnie yelled.

"You're supposed to say that right now. Stop acting like you care about me when you don't!" he said.

"Jordan, I do care about you, and if your grandmother Weida was here, she'd be doing the same thing."

"I wouldn't know, I never met her," he screamed back.

"Well, she was my best friend, Jordan, and I can't let nothing happen to you, so please make the right decision here."

Callie leaned over to grab Titus Klayton.

"I can't say for sure, but I think he has a gun," she whispered with a worried, yet unsure look.

"A gun? And you're just now telling me this!" Titus said. "What do you mean, you *think* he has a gun, Callie?"

"Because he used to take his dad's gun from the lock box all of the time. He used to brag about it," Callie said.

Titus motioned for Miss Minnie to come over.

He said, "Come down here. I need to whisper something to you, Miss Minnie. I don't know for certain, but there's a chance he could have a gun in that bathroom. We need to call the authorities to let them handle this," Titus said.

Shocked at his suggestion, Miss Minnie said, "Titus, this is a community and we do things together. I can't believe you would even suggest something like that. Especially if you ain't even certain if he has one or not."

Titus said, "Miss Minnie, I don't know what to do, I just want to be safe because there are other people in here — my babies are in here and my little brother."

"If we call the police and he does have a gun, it will change the entire course of his life," Minnie said. "Especially with Judge Fox sitting over there. You of all people, Titus Klayton, shouldn't want that boy going through life with a record following him everywhere he goes."

Titus simply gave her a look of agreement as she made her way back to the bathroom door.

Miss Minnie knocked on the door.

"Jordan, Jordan, what do you need, baby? Can I get you anything?"

"Yes you can," Jordan said. "You can start by telling me what's wrong with me."

"What you mean, child? Ain't a single thing wrong with you," Minnie said.

"Then why am I in this bathroom?" Jordan screamed. "And why do I feel so down about myself?"

"Say what?" Minnie said as she started laughing loudly.

"What's so funny?" Jordan yelled through the door.

"I think it's hilarious that you think you're the only one who's been on that side of the bathroom door before."

Minnie started to look around the room at the DMV. She paused long enough to make eye contact with everyone. If someone tried to look away, she stared at them even longer, forcing them to look back.

"Jordan, listen to me, son," Minnie said, as she talked even louder. "Every single one of us out here has had to make this decision at some point in our lives."

"What decision?" Jordan yelled.

"To choose life, son. I'm talking about choosing life. And unfortunately, none of us can make that choice for you. But I promise you this, there are some of us in this room right now who are trying to make that same decision that you need to make right now."

"What?" Jordan said.

"Yep, and many of them are looking into my eyes while I am talking to you right now, Jordan."

As Miss Minnie surveyed the room, she gave special time and attention to each and every person in the room.

When she looked at the Murphy twins, she wondered what challenges they too were facing as teenagers in today's world.

When she locked eyes with Titus Klayton, she looked deeply into his heart, beyond his new-found fame, or the movie deals and the magazines. She saw the young man inside of him that she once knew. She saw the inmate in his eyes, the one who worried if he could ever grow beyond the way some members of society would label him, regardless of his guilt or innocence.

Looking at Judge Frank Fox, Minnie knew that underneath the pinstripe suit and the professional swagger was a man who was as uncertain about himself as he was on the first day of his first semester in law school.

Miss Minnie spent extra time when she glanced at Darla DuVernay. Just starring in Darla's direction was enough to make her boyfriend uncomfortable. Miss Minnie knew that Darla had a big decision of her own to make about the very child she carried in her womb.

With her eyes still focused on Darla, Minnie loudly said, "Remember, Jordan, when you choose life, you choose everything that comes with it. The highs, the lows, the joys and the pain. **But once you choose life, that's where your worry ends and God's mystery begins."**

" *When you chose life, that's where your worry ends and God's mystery begins.* "

Darla DuVernay could NOT hold back her tears any longer. In a sudden outburst, she turned to her boyfriend and yelled as loud as she could, "I'm keeping it, I'm keeping it!"

Startled, the boyfriend said, "Keeping what?"

Towering over top of him as the boyfriend still sat in his seat, Darla continued to yell, "Keeping what? Keeping what? The fact that you even have to ask. I am keeping this baby, with or without you!"

"No you are NOT!" he yelled back.

"Yes I am," she said. "And you can leave if you want to."

The boyfriend stood up, face to face with Darla.

Joe Moscufo immediately jumped out of his chair.

"Hey tough guy, I don't think you want to do that!"

"Mind your business, spaghetti head," the boyfriend screamed.

As Joe Moscufo pushed the boyfriend out of Darla's face, Darla yelled to her boyfriend, "If you walk out of that door now, don't ever look back."

Jordan Banks was still in the bathroom.

"Miss Minnie, Miss Minnie," he said, "Are you still there? What's going on out there?"

"Yes, I am here, baby. We just sitting here, waiting for another person to make the same kind of decision you bout to make."

Miss Minnie yelled back in Darla's direction towards her boyfriend, "What's it gonna be, sir? Is you staying or is you leaving?"

Without even taking one moment to think about it, the boyfriend headed straight out of the front door.

Broken-hearted and defeated, Darla DuVernay almost fell to the floor before Joe Moscufo caught her in his arms.

As she rubbed her stomach and sobbed, Mendy Donner and a few others rushed over to help her.

Miss Minnie reassured Darla, "The hard part is over, baby. Now that you've made your decision, the rest of the mystery is up to God now."

Turning her attention back to Jordan Banks in the bathroom, Miss Minnie placed her hands on the bathroom door to brace herself.

"Jordan, I hope you're ready, 'cause I'm only going to say this to you once, so don't miss it," she said.

"Say what!" he yelled through the door.

"Knock twice if you can hear me clearly Jordan," she said.

"What?" he responded.

"I said, knock twice if you can hear me Jordan, cause I ain't gonna repeat what I'm about to say twice."

After a few seconds of pause went by, the entire DMV sat silently as they awaited Jordan's response.

Then, Jordan knocked twice to acknowledge her request.

"Get ready, son, and listen up, 'cause here it comes," she said.

Everyone else in the DMV also leaned forward in their seats as well. They were all ready for what she had to say.

"Jordan, here comes the speech, and if this don't get you to come out of that bathroom, nothing will."

"I don't need a speech!" he said, "I just want to know what's wrong with me!"

Minnie said, "Jordan, ain't nothing wrong with you, but there is something wrong with humanity today. When Titus told you earlier that your life's purpose is a secret between you and God, and you needed to spend the rest of your life exploring it, he wasn't lying. The problem is, most of us stopped acting like human beings a long time ago, and we can't handle the mystery of God anymore. We act like we need to **know everything** and **have everything** instantly. Ain't no room for God's mystery anymore, because we have technology and devices that can tell us anything that we want, instantly. But our desire to KNOW EVERYTHING right now comes at a cost, and it's destroying human connection. Why y'all think I don't allow those phones in my DMV? I figured I'd at least give y'all one last place in this world where you can remember what it's like to talk to each other, and act like a human being — who knows, maybe even feel something in your hearts again. The best moments in life are passing right by us, because we're so distracted all the time."

Miss Minnie paused for a moment to observe the body language of everyone throughout the room. Then she continued, "I'll give you another example to make you think for a minute. You know them tight-fitting yoga pants you see women wearing nowadays? Imma tell you why they wearing em. Women used to wear long dresses to cover themselves up. Now they wearing those yoga pants in public, in front of perfect strangers. Nowadays men don't even get the mystery of wondering what a woman looks like anymore — *there's no mystery there* — not when women are showing their *cookies, snacks and doughnuts* to every man who wanna look. Women never used to leave the house looking like that before, but I guess it's what they got to do today to get a man's attention, because everyone is so distracted by their phones and no one's paying attention to each other anymore."

Miss Minnie paused for a moment.

Jordan yelled through the door.

"So that's your advice? To stay away from women wearing yoga pants?" he asked.

Some of customers in the DMV weren't sure if it was too soon to laugh at his comment or not. Most laughed anyway.

"No baby," Miss Minnie said, "That's not what I'm saying at all, I'm just getting started. You asked me why YOU were like this, so

I'm just explaining why *all of us* are like this. Some of y'all can't even stand coming into this DMV, because you can't bring your phones in with you. And some parents today, they can't even stand to parent their kids without shoving a phone or a device in front of them — *even at the dinner table* — but a phone will never be a substitute for a parent's undivided love and attention. Technology is making sure that our brains are always turned on and we wonder why our mental health is bad and we're always stressed out. TV programs used to cut off at a certain time at night and people had nothing else to do at that point but to go to sleep. One of the reasons why people's health is so bad today is 'cause they ain't sleeping right — *TVs don't even cut off anymore.* And when when the TVs are turned off, everybody knows that they are still turned on, because you can watch TV on your phone now, whenever you want. You can even watch them shows on the bench if you want to."

Jordan couldn't help himself; he had to interrupt her.

"Watching shows on the bench, what's that, Miss Minnie?"

"Them kids always talking about watching them shows on the bench or something," Minnie said.

Jordan said, "Miss Minnie, do you mean *binge-watching?*"

She said, "Bench-watching, binge-watching, whatever you want to call it — I bet you know what I mean, don't you?"

Jordan Banks laughed on the other side of the door, just low enough for Miss Minnie to hear him.

"Mr. Jordan Banks, did I just hear you laugh?"

Jordan got quiet again, instead choosing not to respond.

"Jordan, we're here for you, no matter what, you know that, don't you? You ain't the only one struggling, son. That's why we got to do this together."

The next noise that came from the bathroom was the click-click sound of the door being unlocked. As the door opened, Miss Minnie rushed into the bathroom to squeeze Jordan in her arms.

As they slowly began to walk out of the bathroom, many of the customers in the DMV had tears in their eyes — *which was the exact type of human experience that Miss Minnie wanted people to feel at her DMV.*

Minnie turned towards Jordan as she held both sides of his face and said, "Jordan, I hate to see you hurting like this, son, God knows I do. But if it took you hurting today to get every person in this room to stop and pay attention to another human being, then it was worth it if you asked me."

Jordan glanced around the room.

With everyone staring back at him, Minnie said, **"Jordan, if you can capture everyone's attention in *HERE*, then imagine what you can do out *THERE*,"** as she pointed out the window. "Jordan, you're more of a leader than you realize. Do you understand me son?"

Jordan didn't have the confidence to respond.

Miss Minnie said, **"Jordan, you're a strong leader who will change this world one day. You just gotta give yourself time to get there, and you gotta remember that everybody has to learn how to fight through bad days and pick themselves up again."**

Joe Moscufo stepped up. He said, "Hey kid, you made it out of the bathroom, now the rest is easy. And if it makes you feel any better, even though I'm an old man, I still go through rough times just like you do. *As a matter of fact....*" Joe Moscufo paused as he looked around. He seemed unsure of what he was about to say and he hesitated before he began to speak again.

You could tell he felt vulnerable in the moment.

Then he continued, "As a matter of fact, I just made a decision to move down south from up north, and I've never felt more uncomfortable in my life. To tell you the truth, I think I'm even scared a little bit, but don't tell nobody I told you that, or you will end up taking that swim that we talked about earlier."

Jordan was surprised to hear that even Joe struggled at times.

"Mr. Moscufo," Jordan said, "if it made you nervous to move down south, why'd you do it then?"

"Because kid, sometimes you gotta *disrupt yourself* if you want to keep growing," Joe said.

"*Disrupt Yourself?*" Jordan repeated. "That sounds a little crazy, why would someone do that on purpose?"

"You just answered your own question, kid. Purpose. When you do things for a reason, on purpose, it doesn't matter how uncomfortable things get, because your reason is bigger than your comfort," Joe said.

" *It doesn't matter how uncomfortable things get, because your reason is bigger than your comfort.* "

Jordan said, "Okay, but isn't the whole point of life about achieving success so that we can live comfortably?"

"Of course you'd say that, kid, look at ya — you're young, you come from a great family and you've had everything handed to ya your whole entire life. Titus Klayton was right about everything he said to you earlier today — at some point you'll realize that being a leader means you gotta lead yourself first. But you can't be comfortable all the time — you gotta be able to **DISRUPT YOURSELF**."

"Oh, okay, I think I get it," Jordan said.

"Of course you *DON'T GET IT* yet, you're sixteen," Joe said. "But you will get it eventually — you'll get it sooner than you realize. Today you chose life kid, and today was your first step towards that *mystery with God thing* that the pretty lady was just talking about. Hey, the only point I was trying to make is this — **we all struggle, kid, and no one is perfect** — but you gotta keep learning and growing."

After a brief pause, everyone in the room stood silent until Titus Klayton spoke up.

"Jordan, he's right. Every one of us in this room is worried about something — most of us are still waking up every day wondering if we're even enough."

"Enough? Enough of what?" Jordan asked.

"Everyone is different," Titus said, "But personally, I wake up every day worried that people will only see me as a convict for the rest of my life because I went to prison. I struggle feeling good enough."

"Even you, Uncle T? You worry about stuff like that? Even though you have your life back, and you're famous and you have a bunch of money?"

Miss Minnie interrupted.

"Boy, you think fame, money and followers bring happiness? Am I the only one in this room who remembers when Biggie said, *Mo Money Mo Problems?*

Everyone was shocked that Miss Minnie even knew who Biggie was. She could tell they didn't believe her.

Minnie said, "Don't look at me like that. Of course I know who Biggie is, I mean he is the greatest rapper, of all time — *The Notorious B.I.G.!*"

Then Miss Minnie turned back towards Jordan as she continued, "**Success without fulfillment is always the ultimate failure,** son, never forget that."

In a sudden shift of energy, Judge Frank Fox slowly stood up, then he began to walk towards Jordan.

"Miss Minnie, if you don't mind," the judge said.

"Of course, Franklin, everyone is welcomed to speak here — everyone, and that includes you Judge Fox."

Turning towards Jordan, Judge Fox said, "I know that you have strong feelings against me, son, but Titus was right in what he shared with you today."

Jordan interrupted him.

"Don't you dare say his name. How could you, after what you did?"

Miss Minnie held Jordan back as he approached the judge with anger. "Jordan, wait, let him finish," Minnie said. "He is a human being just like you and he deserves the same courtesy and respect that we gave you when you were just locked in the bathroom."

Jordan softened his stance.

Judge Fox said, "No, Miss Minnie, I understand. Jordan has every right to feel that way."

Turning back to address Jordan, Judge Fox said, "Son, whether you believe it or not, I was heartbroken when you locked yourself in that bathroom today. But then, I was overjoyed when you came out."

"You were?" Jordan confirmed.

"Yes. Yes I was," he answered.

"Why would you care about me at all?" Jordan asked.

"Because after the amount of lives I've ruined with my bad decisions as a leader in this community, there are many times I've locked myself in that bathroom — but the difference is, I had no one on the other side of the door to be there when I came out."

"You thought about taking your own life? Why?" Jordan asked.

Zach Gaston stepped closer and he placed his hand on Judge Fox's shoulder for comfort.

Every person in that DMV was waiting to hear Judge Fox's answer.

"Why were you in the bathroom?" Jordan asked.

"Because..." Judge Fox began, only to stop his words. He hesitated as he looked around the room before he continued, "You think Titus and AJ's family are the only ones in this room that I've hurt or torn apart? I can look at every single person in this room, and instead of seeing everyone for who they *really* are, all I see are their friends and family members who I've had to send to jail for one reason or another. And that is what makes me feel like a failure. But today, when a little child asked me to color in a coloring book, it was the first time someone looked at me like I was a human being in a very long time."

In a moment of complete solidarity, Jordan placed his hand on the judge's other shoulder as he said, "Well guess what? It's not too late."

"Not too late for what?" the judge asked.

"To rediscover that secret mystery between you and God," Jordan said. "You just gotta think about the good that can come out of it."

Jordan's words were a major contrast to the attitude he had earlier when he locked himself in the bathroom. Titus wheeled closer to Jordan as he grabbed his other hand.

As Jordan leaned over to hug Judge Fox along with Zach Gaston, Miss Minnie also joined in. For a moment, you would have thought that it was Judge Fox who just stepped out of that bathroom and not Jordan Banks.

In a powerful display of raw humanity, the closeness of everyone in that room could not be denied.

As the rest of the group embraced, Miss Minnie broke away as she walked towards Callie Murphy. Miss Minnie reached down to take Callie's phone away from her.

"See what's happening with everyone in this room right now?" Minnie said to Callie. *"This... is why I don't want no phones up in my DMV,"* she said with a smile, as everyone used the brief moment of laughter to lift the energy in the room.

FOR *DISRUPTORS* ONLY

Your PURPOSE *does not have to be a* SECRET.
Disruptors spend time uncovering their gifts, to use their gifts, to serve others.

Jordan came out of the bathroom, safe and unharmed because of the POWER OF COMMUNITY *and kindness.*

Your PRESENCE *could be the key that* UNLOCKS *hope and strength for someone else. So the next time you're in a room with others,* PAY ATTENTION. *Your family, friends and team members may be desperately looking for connection and kindness to help them make it through their darkest moments.*

Scene

13

THE TRUTH ABOUT MEDIA

 MENDY DONNER'S MOMENT

When everyone finished laughing after Miss Minnie placed Callie's phone in the black box, Mendy Donner knew she had something to say. She'd previously sat quietly throughout most of the back-and-forth conversation with Jordan Banks. However, her background and specialized training compelled her to share some insight with Jordan about the negative impact that technology can have on our focus and mental health.

As Mendy approached him, she said, "Jordan, what if I told you that something was wrong with you, *but it wasn't your fault?*"

"Huh?" Jordan responded.

"What if I told you that someone may have done something to you and you didn't know it. Would you feel better?"

"I don't know. I guess, it depends on what it is. Why do you say that?"

"Have you ever heard of a hijacker before?" Mendy asked.

"You mean, like a person who steals from someone?"

"Yes, just like that."

Mendy continued, "There's a part of your brain called the limbic system, it's one of the oldest parts of our brains."

"Okaaaaay," Jordan said.

"It's okay," Mendy said, "I'll make this quick. There's something in the limbic system of your brain called your amygdala. Your amygdala is responsible for helping you survive by responding to bad things around you."

"Oh yeah, like our fight-or-flight response, right?" Jordan said. "We talk about that all the time in bio class."

"Yes. Exactly," she said. "Jordan, when we feel threatened or afraid of something, our amygdala causes us to respond to fear or danger automatically, without even thinking about it."

"How can we react to stuff if we don't even think about it first?" Jordan asked.

"Because your body releases stress hormones that cause you to fight or run away from danger."

"So you're saying that my Amy-thing is broken?"

Mendy smiled. "It's called the amygdala. Say it like this... *Ahh - Mig - Dah - Lah.*"

Jordan repeated, *"Ahhhhh - Mig - Dah - Lah."*

"See, now you've got it," Mendy said. "And no, Jordan, nothing is wrong with your amygdala. But it is being hijacked."

"What? What do you mean, hijacked?" Jordan asked, as he put his fists up in the air like an alien was attacking him.

"Remember when Miss Minnie talked about TVs and cell phones never being turned off?"

"Yeah, the yoga pants thing, right?"

"Yes Jordan, yoga pants. Well, when you come into Miss Minnie's DMV, there are no TVs, radios, or phones turned on, so your brain only has to process normal things, like sounds in the room, or the temperature of the air, or a smile on someone's face."

Jordan said, "Mendy, I thought you were a reporter, not a doctor?"

She said, "Jordan I learned most of this when I was in journalism school at the University of Florida."

"They taught brain stuff like this to reporters?" he said.

"Not exactly, but they did teach us the basics of how to produce stories that capture your attention. And because I always wanted to be *a different kind of journalist,* my friends and I always studied **extra stuff** outside of the classroom. That's when we began to study the effects that the media has on our brains and in our lives."

"You're crazy," Jordan said. "Most people never do extra work unless they get extra credit."

"You're right, but now I'm working on something called the *Truth In Media Project,* it's kind of my life's work."

"Yeah, the *TIM thing* that my Uncle Titus was talking about earlier, right?"

"Correct. Jordan, I'm telling you this for a reason. Media companies make a lot of money by getting your attention, and they know exactly what to do to keep you watching their programs, and the more you watch, the more money they make from advertisers — it's that simple."

" *Media companies make a lot of money by getting your attention. The more you watch, the more money they make.* "

"Is it legal to do that?" he asked.

"Yes, it's perfectly legal. And they aren't necessarily doing anything wrong, by the way," Mendy said.

"Wait a minute, so you're saying they're hijacking my brain and they're making money from it — and you're telling me it's perfectly legal?"

"Jordan, it is legal, and let me explain something to you. I shared my childhood home with a father who was an alcoholic. Thank God for Alcoholics Anonymous, because the 12-step program helped him realize for the first time in his life that he was controlled by fear. Once he became addicted to living in fear at an early age, that's when he turned to alcohol."

Looking confused, Jordan looked at Mindy and said, "I'm sorry, but I don't think I'm following you. What does being addicted to alcohol have to do with any of this?"

Mendy said, **"Because the media also understands that we're addicted to fear, so they use that addiction against us."**

Jordan said, "Wait, but how does the media know what my fears are if they don't even know me?"

She said, "When you see something on TV or in the news that gives you fear or anxiety, those news stories influence how you think, how you feel, what you believe, and ultimately how you act."

Miss Minnie interrupted. "There are two things that everyone of us in here needs to know about the power of stories. First, you need to know that **whatever story you believe is the story that you will live.** And second, your life will be saved by the stories and testimonies that come out of your mouth. **The stories we hear and the stories we tell have the most power to change our lives!"**

Jordan immediately began to connect the dots.

He said, "Hold up, they do all of this just to control us and make money?"

Mendy said, "No Jordan, some media outlets do a good job of being balanced — there's good media out there too. But you need to know that…"

Jordan interrupted her again.

He said, "Wait, you keep talking about TV and the media. *What about social media, how does that affect us?*" He said.

"Depending on how often you use it, social media can actually affect you more than other forms of media, because we've become so addicted to it."

Then, Mendy looked up at everyone else in the DMV. She realized that she had a larger audience than just Jordan.

Joe Moscufo said, **"You're teaching them how to think for themselves, and they need to hear this because most people act like a bunch of sheep.** People don't even think anymore, they just repeat what everyone else does." Realizing he now had the audience's attention, Joe continued by saying, "Does anyone even know what the word *intentional* means?" Looking back at Jordan, Joe Moscufo said, "Hey Jordan, remember earlier when I told you to **disrupt yourself?**"

"Yeah," Jordan responded.

"Remember when you asked me *how* to **disrupt yourself**, and we talked about doing everything on purpose?"

"Yes sir," Jordan said.

"Well, that's it. **Being intentional means thinking before you act, and doing everything on purpose.** Most people can't even tell you why they do what they do. They just do whatever they see other people do, without even thinking about it — you know why? *Because they're sheep.* And if they aren't careful, they'll learn the hard way, because sheep eventually get slaughtered, so pay attention because this woman knows what she's talking about."

Mendy said, "Thank you, Joe. That was nice of you to say."

Then, out of nowhere, Darla DuVernay softly spoke up to get Mendy's attention.

"Mendy, I need your help because I don't want to be a sheep and I don't want to believe everything I hear. I need to learn how to think for myself and for this baby. So what do I need to do first?"

Mendy said, "That's a great question, Darla, but every one of us comes from different backgrounds, so that's tough to answer. I think a great place for anyone to start at, is first, you need to *know your truth*, second, you need to *live your truth*, and third, *don't be offended* by others if they live a truth that's different than yours."

"Thanks, I appreciate that," Darla said. "But you make it sound so easy. Most of us get stuck on the first step because we can't live our truth if we don't know what truth is."

"You're right, Darla," Mendy said.

Looking up at the rest of the group, Mendy turned around and said, "Hey guys, feel free to join in — anyone — because I certainly don't have all the answers."

Then Darla continued, saying, "Mendy, is there anything out there that can teach me how to discover what's true and what isn't? Because the news channels have their version of the truth, and everyone on social media has their version, so we don't know what to believe anymore. And now, some of the big tech companies are censoring information on social media if you say something wrong, and people are being cancelled if they disagree with someone, so how do we even know what's true and what isn't?"

Mendy said, "The only thing you need to know is how to tell the difference between being a *Storyteller and a Storymaker.* Storytellers talk about the past and Storymakers talk about the future. Storytellers and media companies tell you the information that they want you to hear, and they control the narrative because they have the money and the platform to do it. But **Storymakers** are different because **Storymakers** have the courage to discover their own truth so they can think for themselves."

Titus's little brother AJ Klayton sat up a little straighter when he heard Mendy Donner say that. AJ was an aspiring lawyer who dreamed of fighting for people who were victimized by wrongful convictions.

AJ said, "Mendy, can I ask a question? If the people in power control the narrative, and they control what we hear and see, what power do we have to change it?"

"I believe there is something we can do AJ," Mendy said. "But it takes courage. And courage is what our *Truth In Media Project* is all about."

"Courage? What takes courage?" he said.

"You need to have the courage to live your own truth," Mendy said.

"Why does that take courage?" AJ asked. "Don't we do that already?"

"Most of the time we don't because we're handed our identities the day we're born," Mendy said. "We're taught how to eat, how to sleep, how to play, how to pray, we're even taught which college or professional football teams to cheer for. Most of our identity is handed to us the day we are born. But it takes courage to have the emotional intelligence and self-awareness that it takes to be a **Storymaker** and live your own truth — *especially if your truth is different* than what your friends and family believe."

AJ Klayton quickly looked over at his brother Titus. Titus recognized the look. It was the look that AJ often had whenever he learned something that was impactful.

AJ said, "Mendy, I don't mean to beat a dead horse, but what else you got? I know there's more to this, because my friends are always arguing with each other on social media nowadays because everybody believes different truths. I want to make a real difference. What else can you teach me that I can take back to them?"

Mendy looked over at Miss Minnie and smiled, and Miss Minnie knew exactly what her smile was for. These were the exact moments that Miss Minnie wanted to see people have in her DMV. It's why she had the rules in the first place. She wanted people to talk to each other and connect like we're supposed to as humans.

Mendy looked back at AJ and said, "I'm gonna copy one of Miss Minnie's moves that she used earlier when Jordan was in the bathroom."

"What move?" AJ asked.

Mendy said, *"AJ, I'm only gonna give you this speech once, so you better get ready. Now clap twice if you can hear me."*

Jordan and Miss Minnie both laughed.

AJ stood motionless without responding.

Mendy said, *"AJ... clap twice if you can hear me now!"*

He obliged with a brief *clap clap!*

"Okay, here I go," Mendy said. "In the old days, all human beings used three basic steps to process information. **Step one** was simple — a person's brain would take in sights and sounds from the environment. **Step two**, the person took time to process what they saw or heard, and they didn't just respond automatically. And in **Step three**, depending on what they observed, they made a thoughtful, intelligent decision based on the information their brain analyzed. But most importantly, **all humans used to take the time to think before they responded**.

"Humans aren't the only ones that do this; animals do it too. Their brains use similar input mechanisms to process information before they commit to a behavior.

"The difference with humans today is, because **our brains are constantly connected to technology** like Miss Minnie explained to us earlier, they have more information to analyze than ever before, and our brains are overloaded. But, our brains still want to protect us from danger around us, so they're forced to respond faster, because we have so much going on in our heads. But, our brains must be efficient. So to process the overwhelming amount of information, sometimes we skip steps without knowing it and without even thinking about what we're doing."

AJ Klayton said, "But I thought you told Jordan that our amygdala processes all of those decisions for us, without even thinking?"

"It does, AJ, but we're skipping the *critical thinking part* because that happens mostly in another part of our brain called the prefrontal cortex, the part that helps us control our responses and our behavior."

When Mendy finished that sentence, everyone in the room looked like they were paralyzed with information overload.

Mendy followed up with, "Listen guys, let's move on to something else because I can tell that...."

Jordan interrupted her again, "No, no, no, this was just starting to make sense to us — don't stop now."

Others joined in, encouraging her to continue.

Mendy said, "Okay, I guess I will finish by saying this: today, our brains are making faster, more emotionally-based decisions because our brains are tired from always being connected to technology. That's why we skip steps like thinking critically before we make decisions. And that's why there's so much arguing and tension throughout the world today."

"So you're saying we need to slow down and think about stuff first before we act — is that what I'm hearing?" AJ said.

"Exactly, AJ. That's why it's so easy to **disagree with someone**, or **cancel someone**. Because it's fast and it's easy for our brains to process that type of decision because it takes extra time and effort to develop empathy and compassion for someone who thinks differently than you."

Joe Moscufo jumped back in. "Ohhhh, now I get it. Is that why people are so **easily offended** today?"

Mendy said, "Joe, always remember, our brains just want to process information and help us survive. Developing empathy for others and forcing yourself to not be easily offended takes effort. **And lazy people don't like effort.** It's just easier for them to **cancel** you, or **discredit** you, and **move on**."

Titus Klayton asked, "Mendy, what if someone cancels you but people later realize they were wrong? If the damage has already ruined your reputation, what can you do about it then?"

"Titus, as you told Jordan earlier, unfortunately that's what it means to choose life," Mendy said. "Things aren't always fair, and we will never be able to control what other people do. But real Storymakers rise above lies and drama because they don't need to control others to live their own truth."

Miss Minnie said, "Ohhhh child, you preaching today. But I have a question. What exactly can we do to be better *critical thinkers?*

Mendy said. "Just remember that you need to **observe** and **interpret** information before you take steps to **apply** it."

Miss Minnie said, "Child, this sounds good, but Imma need you to break some of this down for me."

Mendy Donner smiled and blushed at the request.

After pausing for a moment, Miss Minnie said, "Oh no, I wasn't just trying to flatter you, I was being serious," as she pointed Mendy towards the white board to write on.

Mendy hesitated at first, but once her hands took over, the information started pouring out of her as she drew the following chart on the board:

STEP 1	STEP 2	STEP 3
OBSERVE	**INTERPRET**	**APPLY**
BE OPEN	BE SELF-AWARE	TRUST YOUR GUT
DON'T JUDGE	HONEST SELF-TALK	ACT INDEPENDENTLY OF FRIENDS & FAMILY
DO YOUR OWN RESEARCH	THINK INDEPENDENTLY	TAKE RISKS
DISCUSS & DEBATE OPPOSITE OPINIONS	LET YOUR VALUES GUIDE YOU NOT EMOTION	LIVE & SHARE YOUR TRUTH
LISTEN CLOSELY NO INTERRUPTING	INTERRUPT "CANCEL" OLD IDEAS WITH NEW ONES	HAVE RESPECT & EMPATHY AS OTHERS LIVE THEIRS

After she was finished, Mendy said, "I was professionally trained to be a Storyteller. But what the world needs most is people who know how to be **Storymakers**. This chart will help you **observe, interpret** and **apply** truth to your life without making emotional choices that are harmful to yourself and others."

She turned back to the rest of the group and said, "Listen everyone, the media really does need to be more responsible for the content they produce, but ultimately, you have to be responsible for the information that you consume. Every time you use an app on your phone, almost everything you do is being tracked and analyzed, then your data is sold by big tech companies to advertisers."

Miss Minnie jumped right back in.

"See I knew it, I knew it, I knew it. These phones tracking everything we do, they ain't nothing but the anti-Christ, they ain't nothing but the devil."

Everyone laughed.

Mendy said, "Miss Minnie, we should be thanking you. This DMV is one of the last places where we can connect with different people, from different backgrounds, without being distracted. And you're helping us to remember what it feels like to be human beings again. Thank you, Miss Minnie!"

" This DMV is one of the last places where we can connect with people without being distracted. "

Titus Klayton pushed his wheelchair over to get closer to Miss Minnie as he grabbed her hand.

The Murphy twins, Addie and Callie, jumped up to hug her too as they shared their appreciation.

Everyone inside of the Clairmont DMV began to clap and cheer for Miss Minnie as they praised her.

Embarrassed, and never looking for acknowledgement, Miss Minnie quickly tried to quiet everyone down.

"Y'all need to quit. Stop all that," she said. "The good Lord gave us a perfectly good brain, so if we act right and use it every now and then, instead of using these phones so much, God will take care of the rest."

Then Miss Minnie hugged Mendy Donner again as she said, "Mendy, you have a gift and you are more talented than you realize. You do more than just tell good stories. Today you taught every one of us in here how to be Storymakers ourselves by finding our own truth. Your *Truth In Media Project* is going to change the world someday."

FOR *DISRUPTORS* ONLY

ATTENTION IS EXPENSIVE.

Many corporations make large profits by getting your attention. Which means, everything that you give your attention to, costs you something. The question is, "How much are you worth?"

Disruptors are strong enough to **TUNE OUT DISTRACTIONS** *and tune in for better results.*

If you don't like your results, it may have nothing to do with how talented you are. So do yourself a favor — **PUT YOUR PHONE DOWN** *— so you can pick your* **DREAMS** *up. Because you can't hold them both in the same hand.*

Scene

14

THE DISRUPTION MODEL

Before Emmett and Avery knew it, their flight had already landed in Atlanta and they were boarding their connecting flight to Charleston, South Carolina. The brief flight from Atlanta to Charleston would take less than thirty-five minutes, and Emmett knew that he had less than two hours before the event started.

"Relax, Emmett," Avery said. "If the plane takes off on time, which it looks like it should, we'll make it there just in time for the event."

"I hate going to events like this," Emmett said.

"Like what? Events where people are at? Or events that you may be late for?"

"No, I hate going to events where I don't know why I'm there in the first place," he said.

"Well, if we learned anything about this Miss Minnie lady, she's a tough old bird but she has a big heart for people," Avery said. Then she looked at him with a strong "*I know I'm always right*" *type of look*, and she said, "I think your mom did the right thing by making you come to this ceremony for Miss Minnie, and I'm glad I came too."

Emmett said, "Well, speaking of Claire Cooper," as he looked down to read a text she sent.

/// FROM GM EVER — 2 hours to go. Don't be late. Meet you there.

Followed by another text that said.

/// FROM GM EVER — btw, I will save you a seat... up front :)

Claire was the type of parent who would be okay with her son if he shot someone or robbed a bank — because she'd always love him no matter what. But, if Emmett violated one of *Momma's Special Rules,* as Claire called them, he would be dead — and one of her most important rules was *sitting in the front row.*

Thinking about *Momma's Special Rules* reminded Emmett of Miss Minnie, which switched his mind back to the story they had quickly become obsessed with.

Emmett turned to Avery and said, "Hey, it looks like there's not much of the story left to read. Do you want to just wait to finish reading it tonight?"

"Are you kidding me? Let's finish it now!" she demanded. "We have another forty-five to fifty minutes to go and hopefully later tonight your mother can tell us what this story is all about."

Like a smart man, Emmett was already intelligent enough to know that women were always right.

~~~~~~~~~~

THE DISRUPTION MODEL

Jordan's father, Dorian Banks, finally arrived back at the DMV after taking a brief timeout to check on things at work. Before he walked back in, he passed Cork Howard and the other reporters who were still waiting outside of the DMV to interview Titus Klayton.

"Good luck in there," Cork said. "I couldn't really hear what they've been saying in there, but I can see 'em through the window, and things look pretty interesting in there."

"Interesting? What do you mean by that?" Dorian asked.

"It looks like it did when New Edition was deciding if they wanted to kick Bobby Brown out of the group or not," Cork said.

"Huh?" Dorian said.

"You know, before he met Whitney Houston — *that Bobby Brown*," Cork said.

Dorian just laughed as he walked inside, but he couldn't help but think to himself, *Bobby Brown?*

Walking in the door, Dorian Banks knew that the energy in the room was different, but he had no idea that he was walking into a social autopsy as the entire room participated in a post-mortem evaluation about *what's wrong with humanity today.*

When Jordan Banks saw his father walk in, he immediately ran to hug him, and Dorian knew right away that the hug felt unfamiliar. Of course he'd hugged his son before, but this felt different — there was a strong connection when they embraced, stronger than before.

Titus and Dorian made eye contact while Dorian was still hugging his son Jordan. Titus motioned for Dorian to come and sit beside him.

Dorian said, "TK, what's going on in here? Something feels different," as he noticed the quiet room starring back at him.

"Just some good ole-fashioned conversation with friends," Titus said.

Dorian thought to himself, *friends?* as he noticed how closely Judge Frank Fox was sitting near Titus and his family. He also noticed that no one was standing in line at the DMV. Everyone was seated, and Miss Minnie and Pastor Eddie weren't behind the counter. They were standing near Mendy Donner by the white board. Dorian also couldn't miss the vibe that was coming from Joe Moscufo, as his tall, New York City Italian presence stood closely by.

Dorian Banks always noticed everything — which was a skillset he developed early on. He also realized that Darla DuVernay was now sitting alone, without her boyfriend.

"Did I miss something?" Dorian said directly to Miss Minnie, as he looked around the room once more.

"Don't you come in here asking no questions," Minnie said. "You lucky I let you back into my DMV, and you better tell me that y'all got those planes back up in the air too," she said with her hands on her hips, actually expecting to hear that Dorian single-handedly fixed a global fleet of aircrafts, that fast.

Of course, everybody laughed.

Titus knew that there was something he needed to share while he still had the group's attention. His words cut straight through the air like the sound of a smartphone crashing to the floor. *Yeah, that sound —*

the sound that's only okay when you KNOW that it's someone else's phone.

Titus said, "After listening to everything that we've talked about today, there's one thing that I forgot to share."

He had everyone's attention.

He continued, "You all need to know that going to prison was the best thing that ever happened to me."

The room didn't really know how to respond to that, especially since it was such a sudden transition in conversation.

"I had to go to prison to find myself," Titus Klayton said. "Before I was arrested, I was so busy being a sheep, just like Joe Moscufo described, that **I had no idea who I was.** Before prison, my entire identity was handed to me, just like Mendy said. From the day I was born, I was told who I was and what I believed and I never discovered what I valued or believed on my own. But in prison I had time to sit and think for the first time ever. I realized that the most important things in this world, outside of my relationship with God, are love and discipline."

At that moment, Dorian Banks was thinking to himself *exactly what did I miss when I was gone?*

Titus continued, "That's right, even though it wasn't fair that I was sent to jail, I still had a chance to learn how to love myself first. Having self-love is why I can give empathy and respect to others now, because **I learned to love myself first.**"

As Titus pointed directly at Joe Moscufo, he said, "Hey, this guy was right when he said that we needed to **disrupt ourselves.** Prison disrupted me and it forced me to get uncomfortable, but that's when my life changed."

Another voice in the back of the room spoke up.

"Excuse me, excuse me," the soft, unfamiliar voice said with a foreign accent.

Everyone turned towards her. Her smile was alluring and her presence was absolutely undeniable. She was also beautiful, beautiful in a way that made others in the room immediately wonder who she was and why they had not noticed her until this moment.

The woman spoke up and said, "Titus is right. I came to America like most people, looking for an opportunity to learn and grow. And forgive me for saying but...." the woman hesitated as she looked around the room.

Miss Minnie gracefully said, "It's okay. Go ahead, baby. Everybody's welcome in here."

She continued as she said, "Titus is correct, because the first thing me and my family noticed when we arrived in America was how undisciplined the people were. In my country, God is first, followed by family, education and hard work. We practice each of those with great discipline. But it breaks my heart to see people in this country take things for granted by giving such a poor effort, with little discipline and self-control."

"Hey, what's your name?" Titus asked.

Afraid of the possibility that she may have offended someone, she answered a little softer.

"Jaha Fatou. My name is Jaha Fatou," she said.

Joe Moscufo said, "Oh, West African, right?"

She smiled back with amazement that Joe knew that.

"Yes, yes I am," she said.

"What part?" Joe asked.

"I am from Gambia," she said. "And where I am from, the smartest, most educated kids are the most celebrated. Our school grades are posted in public for everyone to see, because that's what we celebrate. We compete with education like Americans compete with athletics, because in my country if you are born poor, there's a great chance that you will die poor and it is very hard to break out of the social class you are born into. That's why faith, discipline and education is very important to us. In America we have the opportunity to use our discipline and education to succeed with no limits."

AJ said, "West Africans are highly ranked as some of the most successful immigrants in the U.S. — now I understand why."

Joe Moscufo responded, "If you don't mind me saying, I think you are the most beautiful woman I've ever seen."

Jaha smiled and simply said, "You are very kind."

Miss Minnie said, "Ummm hmmm."

"What?" Joe Moscufo said. "My wife Carol and I are old now — we just call it like we see it. Look at her, she's beautiful."

Jaha Fatou stepped forward to hand Titus something on a piece of paper.

"What is this?" Titus asked.

"It's a model," she said.

"A model, what kind of model?" he asked.

"It's a **DISRUPTION MODEL**," she confirmed.

Jordan Banks said, "Disruption Model? What is that?" as he leaned in to view the piece of paper Titus was holding.

"It's everything we've been talking about today," Jaha said. "Mr. Joe Moscufo said that you needed to **disrupt yourself** if you wanted to grow. This model might help."

AJ Klayton asked her, "What are you, some type of doctor-reporter genius, just like Mendy Donner?"

"No, I am a data engineer," Jaha said. "I study data to find predictable patterns. And today I sat in the back of the room as I listened to everything that each of you had to say. I began to analyze the patterns and this is what I came up with."

Joe Moscufo said, "Hey, you been writing down my words all day? Be careful, pretty lady. They make tiny cement shoes too."

Jordan Banks jumped in to have some fun too.

"Relax, Mr. Moscufo," he said with a smile. "You only have enough cement for my shoes anyway!"

Jaha said, "This model will guarantee that any person, team or organization can predict to a degree of certainty their future growth by focusing on two areas, **comfort and discipline.**"

She walked to the white board where Mendy Donner was standing.

"May I, for a moment please?" she asked.

"Sure. Girl power — go get em!" Mendy said.

In a very slow and methodical manner, Jaha Fatou slowed down her words as she said, *"Now, I'm only going to tell you this once..."*

The place erupted in laughter.

Dorian Banks was the only one who didn't get it.

Then Jaha said, "Next, I am supposed to say... *clap twice if you hear me.*"

They laughed even more and then she got an immediate *clap, clap* returned from everyone.

Then she began her speech by saying, "Joe Moscufo said that we need to **disrupt ourselves** and he was right. That's also what Mendy taught us to do with truthful information. She taught us how to **disrupt ourselves** by discovering truth for ourselves."

Looking at Titus, she continued, "Titus Klayton, you did not **disrupt yourself** when you went to prison, but you were disrupted, so you still experienced tremendous growth."

She turned towards Dorian Banks and she said, "You were also **disrupted,** Dorian Banks, when you lost your parents at an early age — you developed increased levels of emotional intelligence, self-awareness, empathy and compassion for others — which is why you still visit hospitals and homeless shelters today."

Dorian Banks, said, *"Wait.. How do you..."*

Titus interrupted Dorian.

"It's okay, big brother — we covered a lot while you were gone."

Jaha Fatou continued by saying, "**This Disruption Model only requires two simple things — COMFORT and DISCIPLINE.** This model only needs two data points to get an accurate prediction of whether your will be **DISRUPTED** or if you will be the **DISRUPTOR**."

Miss Minnie said, "Baby, the Lord gave you all that just by sitting and listening to us today."

"Yep," Jaha said, as she leaned over to hug Miss Minnie and added, "it's amazing what can happen when we put our phones down and talk to each other, right, Miss Minnie?"

(see the Disruption Model on the next page)

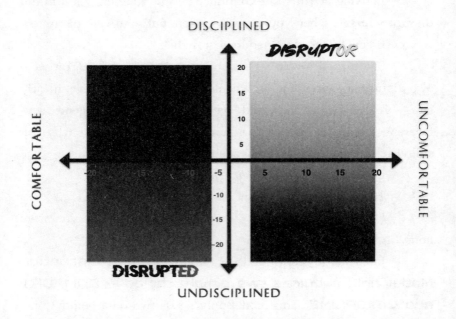

Scene

15

COMFORT OR DISCIPLINE

Dorian Banks knew that he missed something special when he left the DMV earlier in the day. He also knew that the woman standing in front of him was brilliant.

"Excuse me, Jaha. Can I ask you a quick question about this new Disruption Model you created?" he asked.

"Of course, as long as you realize that I may not have the answer you are looking for," Jaha Fatou said.

"As an athlete, our coaches used to teach us new plays all the time. The plays were simple, but it always took some practice before it became automatic. So if we want to shift our *comfort and discipline*, where should we start?"

She said, "First we must all understand that our brains have evolved over two million years. That means unfortunately we are dealing with **two-million-year-old survival software** that is hard-wired. The only way to upgrade our mindset programming is with new experiences. **So you must disrupt yourself, because discipline does not come automatically.**"

Dorian asked, "So is there a difference when we are tying to change the habits of one person versus changing the habits of a team, family or organization?"

"Well, my primary work is with organizations and teams," Jaha said, "but I have discovered that **all work should begin with the individual, then end at the community or team level.**"

As soon as she said the word *community*, Joe Moscufo shifted his stance and he smiled a little.

Dorian asked, "So where should individuals start then?"

"That depends on the **disciplines** you want to grow," Jaha said. "So let's ask around."

Looking at the entire group standing in the DMV, she said, "What does everyone think are the major issues facing our world today, that people need to become more disciplined in?"

Initially, everyone was hesitant to speak up. So Jaha said, "Let's think about it like this: when I look at data to find predictable patterns of behaviors, first I start with inputs, because our input will always determine our output. So based on our conversation today, we discussed several of those inputs that we need to be more disciplined in."

Mendy Donner spoke up. "Information. We need to manage the information that we take in, because that's what determines our **thoughts, habits and behaviors.**"

Jaha wrote **TRUTHFUL INFORMATION** on the board.

All of a sudden, from the back of the room, one of the reporters from the outside walked through the door.

"Oh that's easy," he said. "Food. People need to manage their food input because that's what's killing us more than anything else."

Miss Minnie said, "Now, Mr. Courtney Howard, what did I tell you reporters about being inside of my DMV? You know my rules."

Cork said, "Sorry, Miss Minnie, but I could tell something deep was happening in here, so I took my reporter hat off. I'm here as a regular citizen."

Miss Minnie said, "Well you got me there. Ain't much I can say to you bout that. At least take a seat then."

Jaha Fatou wrote the words **FOOD & DIET** on the board.

"What else?" Jaha said.

Jordan Banks spoke up. "I guess we should think about our technology input. If we don't, everyone will be too connected and distracted, and there are just some people that I do NOT want to see walking 'round in yoga pants."

"Jordan Banks, stop it," his father said.

Jaha wrote the words **TECHNOLOGY INPUT** on the board.

"Anything else?" Jaha Fatou asked.

"Hey, shouldn't we put something up there about community or human connection?" Joe Moscufo asked.

Jaha wrote **COMMUNITY & CONNECTION** on the board.

She said, "Let's stop for a moment and start with those four items. If we had to rank **information, food, technology and community** in order, based on how much they impact our lives — which order should we rank them in?"

Titus Klayton really sat up straight when she asked that question. This was where he shined the most, because the first thing that was disrupted in his life when he went to jail was his **diet.**

Titus said, "Our **relationship with food** drives us more than anything else in the world."

"What?" asked his little brother AJ Klayton. "That's a big statement — how could you say we should rank that first? We should rank **TRUTHFUL INFORMATION** first because that includes everything we read, even the Bible, and you can't tell me that food is more important than God."

Jaha Fatou said, "AJ, we aren't talking about what's more important, because different people believe certain things are more important than others. What you should focus on are the individual disciplines driving human behavior the most, and food is a major driver."

Titus added, "That's because people aren't just addicted to food, we are addicted to the glucose that we get from the food we eat."

AJ argued, "What? That's not true. How can you say that we should rank food higher than God?"

Titus said, "Of course food isn't more important that God. But do yourself a favor. Go three days without praying to God, then go three days without eating. After that, you will know which one controls your life the most."

"Go three days without praying and go three days without eating. Then, you'll realize how much food controls you. "

Many people immediately shook their heads in agreement.

"God is important," Titus said. "God is most important to me, but we are talking about being disciplined, not mindful."

The analogy was so simple that everyone agreed with it, whether they wanted to or not.

Cork Howard said, "I got stuck in an elevator once. I almost ate my brother's leather shoe, *and that was just one day.*"

Jaha put **FOOD & DIET** in the first position on the board.

"What should be next?" she said.

Jordan added, "It would have to be **TECHNOLOGY**, instead of information and community, because we use technology to get our information and to find out what's going on in the community."

The group agreed.

Mendy Donner said, "**TRUTHFUL INFORMATION** would have to be next, then, followed by community."

Jaha Fatou asked the group, "Does anyone have any issues with this order?" After seeing no objections, she ranked the list on the board.

> 1. FOOD
> 2. TECHNOLOGY
> 3. TRUTHFUL INFORMATION
> 4. COMMUNITY

Dorian Banks said, "Okay, so now all we have to do is run each of these disciplines through the disruption model, right?"

"Precisely," Jaha said. "The next step is to list strategies that we can use to disrupt ourselves for each one. Any ideas for what we can do to disrupt ourselves with food?"

"Yeah, we need to stop drinking and eating dairy," AJ Klayton said. "Think about it — we're the only animals that eat or drink another animal's milk, which is supposed to be growth hormone for baby cows."

Everyone laughed.

AJ said, "No, I'm serious. Disease in the body starts with inflammation — all disease, even cancer. The proteins in dairy cause tons of inflammation, and milk is actually bad for most humans, but advertisers will never tell you that directly."

Mendy Donner said, "That's all a part of having access to truthful information. We need to know these things."

Joe Moscufo said, "Or… your neighbor could slap you on the head every time they see you doing something stupid, just in case you didn't read about it somewhere. That's what I call community!"

Titus said, "When I went to prison I wanted to learn everything I could about **FOOD & DIET**. First I learned that in Europe and other places, people are healthier because their governments don't allow certain types of chemicals in their food. So we need to eat more fruits, vegetables and fresh food. The less processed food we eat, the better."

Miss Minnie said, "Baby, my grandparents, great-grandparents and my great-great-grandparents all lived to be at least one hundred years old because they ate fresh food straight from the farms they lived on, so Titus is right about that."

Titus added, "The most important thing we need to do is reverse our **relationship with food**. Our desire to eat controls us, but we need to control it. Just because you feel hungry doesn't mean you need to eat — most of the time we just eat because it's an addiction."

Darla DuVernay said, "Well now I will be eating for two, so I won't be able to help it," as everyone laughed with support.

Titus added, "Have any of you ever heard of Dr. Valter Longo? He works at Southern Cal University."

The Murphy twins Addie and Callie both jumped to their feet. "Oh we have, we have. My uncle is a professional speaker and he teaches people how to be healthier and have more motivation in life. He told us that Dr. Longo is the guy who studied intermittent fasting right?"

Titus said, "Wow. I'm impressed. Listen, intermittent fasting is simple: you just pick an eight-hour eating window, for instance from twelve noon to eight at night, and you only eat food during that time period."

Joe Moscufo said, "And skip breakfast? Are you out of your mind?"

"No, you don't skip breakfast. You just eat it at 12:00pm noon, instead of in the morning" Titus said. "And you can still have coffee or tea in the morning, but you can't put milk, sugar or butter or anything in it, because that will trigger your body's digestive response, and take you out of the fasting phase. You also can NOT have any orange juice, smoothies, etc. before you break your fast at noon."

"I'm not eating eggs and pancakes at lunch," Joe said.

"No, the word breakfast literally means *break your fast.*" Titus said, "First, Dr. Longo did multiple studies where he gave animals the same amount of food on the same day. The only difference was that the *FASTING* group of animals only eat food during eight-hour periods, but he let the *AMERICAN* group eat all day long (just like each of us are doing already). At the end of the study, the American group weighed 25% more, and they had more diseases and illnesses."

Jordan Banks said, "Wait a minute, both groups ate the same amount of food, on the same day, but the fasting group was healthier? Why was that?"

Titus said, "First of all, because when we are not eating, our body goes into a phase called *autophagy*. Autophagy is when your cells automatically heal themselves, which makes your body super healthy and primed for awesomeness. Our bodies can't go into autophagy mode when we are eating because our body is focused on digesting and processing food at that time. For most people who eat all day long, even if you eat small meals, the only time your body goes into autophagy mode is when we are sleeping for five to eight hours. People who fast intermittently give their bodies a chance to grow and become even healthier for sixteen hours, instead of only five to eight hours while they sleep."

Dorian Banks added in, "And, there's the fact that our two-million-year-old brain is used to searching for food because we had to fast while we looked for food."

Titus said, "That's exactly right, Dorian. We always went periods of time without food while we searched for more. But today, we don't have to hunt or search for food; we just get as much of it as we want at the supermarket and we put it in the refrigerator where it sits until we're ready to eat it. So that's why we need to disrupt ourselves and have more self-control with our food addictions, or our *relationship with food* will control us."

Jaha Fatou was extremely proud of the input she was getting from the group. She was also a *realist* — she knew that the entire vision for the model wouldn't be finalized in a few minutes in the middle of a DMV. But she was still proud to see that something so simple could spark such great ideas — which was her only point. She didn't expect to solve all the world's problems in a few moments, but she did know that all solutions to all problems began with effort.

Jaha said, "So, as Titus just taught us, if we are willing to be uncomfortable with our relationship with food and have more self-control, that discipline will help us become healthier."

Callie Murphy stepped and said, "So, every time we try something new, even if it's uncomfortable at first, our numbers will increase on the model, right?"

"Yes, exactly," Jaha said.

Callie stepped up to the front of the room. She grabbed the marker and placed a 1, 2, 3 and 4 on each quadrant of the model.

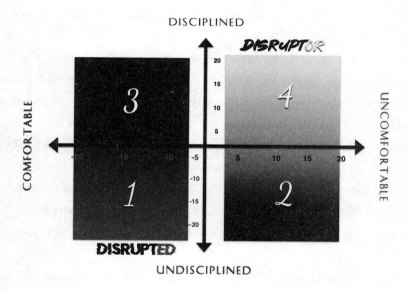

Callie's twin sister Addie spoke up from her seat. She said, "What my sister is trying to say is that every beginner starts in quadrant 1, but as we get **more uncomfortable** and **grow our disciplines,** we make progress, and if we're consistent, we can all make it to quadrant 4 and become disruptors."

"Wow," Jaha said. "It looks like my job here is done," as the rest of the group laughed.

Dorian Banks said, "Wait a minute — shouldn't every model produce a result? Let's put the results up there."

Jaha Fatou said, "That's the easy part. **The results always take care of themselves when we make the effort.** The hard part is just being honest with ourselves, but this model is all about effort and accountability."

Titus said, "If we shared this information with our friends and families at home, how could we sell it to them? I mean, in this example with Food, Technology, Information and Community, what would the results be?"

Jaha said, "How does this look?" As she began to write the results on the board, she said, "If we disrupt ourselves and create better disciplines with **food and technology**, we will be *healthier* and have more *energy*. If we disrupt ourselves with how we access **truthful information**, we will produce our own *certainty and hope* instead of relying on others to tell us how to think, and if we create better **community** among us, we will create better *human connection*."

Dorian said, "But we didn't go over any of the strategies for being more disciplined with technology and truthful information yet."

"Of course we did," Jaha said with a smile. "That's what we talked about day long, but you were at Boeing solving all the world's airline problems, remember?"

Once again, the group couldn't help but laugh.

Joe Moscufo said, "I have the best example in the world for what we can do to drive community. Everybody needs to hear this."

"Okay, Mr. Moscufo," Jaha said. "But before you do, let me finish updating the model with the results that Dorian asked to see."

It was simply amazing. After looking at the results on the Disruption Model, the group realized in that moment just how far they came in one day.

Pastor Eddie said, "In all of my years working here at this DMV with Miss Minnie, I have seen just about all that you can imagine, but I've never seen anything like this. All we did was have conversations with each other, and look what we've come up with — this model is something that can help everybody."

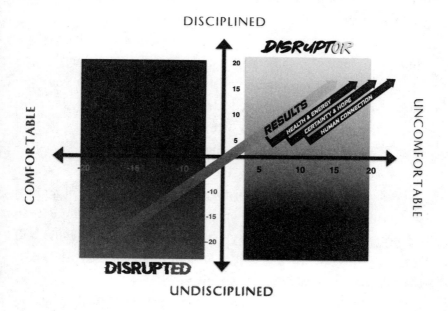

He turned to give Miss Minnie a hug and said, "Miss Minnie, you're a genius. Thank you for being so strict with your rules."

Once again, everyone started clapping and praising Miss Minnie for her vision and leadership.

Miss Minnie said, "Y'all need to take this model home and use it with your families and friends — heck, you can even use it at work to make sure you aren't being too comfortable there. But if you do use it with your companies, just know two things. First, **the job of every leader is to create an environment for the team to get focused so they can connect and share with each other; if they do that the results will always come**. But the second thing you need to know is this — if you make any money from the stuff I've taught you, then I get a 5% royalty off the profits!"

Joe Moscufo said, "You are right, Miss Minnie — all it takes is a little bit of connection and the rest of the magic will happen!"

Looking around the room, he said, "Have any of you ever heard of something called the *Roseto Effect*?"

Everyone looked at him with empty faces.

"Wow, none of yah, not a single one?" he said.

He continued, "I know I'm in the south now, but it's time y'all got an Italian-American history lesson. So I'll make it simple: back in the '40s, '50s and '60s there was a small Italian community in a place called Roseto, Pennsylvania, right between Philly and Scranton. Now the town is still there today, but you need to know why this place was made famous many years ago.

"People in Roseto were much healthier than anywhere else in the United States. They had less issues of heart disease and stroke and not a single person under fifty ever died of a heart attack there. Everywhere else in the U.S., people were dying thirty-five percent faster than anyone in Roseto. So of course, Johnny Blue and Uncle

Sam had to come and investigate. They sent their best state and federal health investigators, and for seven years, they studied everything we did — how much food we ate, how much alcohol we drank, how many cigars and cigarettes we smoked — and remember, this was in the '60s, way back before doctors even believed that cigarettes could kill you — so believe me when I tell you, *we smoked a lot of cigarettes.*

"We didn't have a bunch of money, so the food we ate was horrible. We couldn't afford the fancy cuts of meats and we couldn't even afford to buy fish, so we ate the worst meat available. We used it to make meatballs, sausages and pasta. Almost half of our diet was the worst kind of fat you can imagine, and we cooked everything in lard... *are you kidding me? Lard?*

"For seven years they poked and prodded us. They went everywhere we went, and they wrote down everything we did. They even wanted samples from us when we went to the bathroom. And no matter what they did... *they could not find a thing.* They had no idea why we were healthier and living longer than everyone else in America. Seven years with Uncle Sam's brightest scientists from Harvard and Yale and nothing. Finally, they realized the *one thing* that they didn't seem to understand about our Italian culture at the time... *how close we were* — and I mean, we were *close.*

"We were a real community and we did everything together — I mean everything. We ate breakfast, lunch and dinner together, we worked in the slate quarries and mines together — and you can't imagine how many people were getting sick and dying from the toxins in those quarries — but not us, not the men and women from Roseto. It took seven years for those researchers to realize that our love, closeness and human connection, and the way we lived in community with each other, was the main reason why we lived longer than everyone else in America. When they realized that, they actually wrote that in their final report. **It was our closeness and our love for one another that caused us to live longer.**"

Addie and Callie both spoke up at the same time.

"No, you go first," Addie said.

Callie said, "Mr. Moscufo, did they have phones back then?"

He said, "What do you think kid?"

"Ummm, maybe?" she said.

"Remember, little lady, we were poor," Joe said, "so we only had one or two phones that everybody used if we needed anything. But we *NEVER* needed anything because we had each other."

Callie looked directly at her sister Addie.

Joe said, "Look, *yous twos* are twins and you can't even imagine sharing the same smart phone, can you?"

They both looked anxious at just the thought of sharing a phone with each other.

Joe said, "Maybe I'm new here, and maybe I don't know nuttin, but why don't we try that here?"

"What?" Addie said, *"Try sharing phones?"*

Joe Moscufo laughed.

"Yes, that too, I guess. But not just phones, everything." Looking at the entire group gathered at the DMV, Joe said, "Why don't we try it right here, right where we live today. Let's share everything with each other like they did in the old days."

Still confused about his suggestion, everyone looked around the room. It seemed like everyone was just waiting for the first person to speak up.

"**You mean like they did in Roseto?**" Jordan asked.

"Exactly," Joe Moscufo said. "Miss Minnie already started us out with this great place — probably the only DMV in the world where people are still talking to each other. Who says we can't take this experience *outside* of the DMV?"

He looked around the room for volunteers.

Joe said, "Listen, there's already a small group of us — that's all we need. **You can do anything with a small group of people if their hearts are in it.**"

"*You can do anything with a small group of people if their hearts are in it.*"

Then, looking directly at Darla DuVernay, Joe said, "Hey, we can face anything together — *anything*," as he looked down at her pregnant stomach. While still looking at her, he said, "We'll be right there to help you with that baby — you'll have a small group of people supporting you — *no matter what*."

Darla DuVernay began to cry even more.

Titus Klayton, Mendy Donner and Judge Fox began to smile and shake their heads up and down in a *yes* motion.

Jordan Banks said, "What would that look like? I mean, what would we do and how would we do it, Mr. Moscufo?"

He said, "Hey kid, listen — **that's what's wrong with people today, all they ever worry about is how. The how is the easy part as long as your heart's in it.**"

"I guess so," Jordan responded.

Then Joe said, "Hey, when Noah started building the ark, he didn't wait for his paisanos to show up. He started with the first piece of wood, so how about this… *dinner on me, tomorrow at my place, everyone's invited.* Why don't we start there?"

There was an instant agreement among everyone. Within a few moments, everyone started to make a list of who was bringing what to dinner.

Joe said, "Hey, hey, hey, maybe you didn't understand me. I said, *dinner is on me, at my place.* What yous guys making a list for?"

Miss Minnie jumped in front of him with her hands on her hips and said, "Because, Joe Moscufo, you're up in here acting just like a typical man. You invited a house full of people to dinner at your place, without even checking with your wife Carol first, so we're making a backup plan just in case!"

All Joe Moscufo could do was smile.

As always… once again, *Miss Minnie was right.*

FOR *DISRUPTORS* ONLY

True disruptors know that ACCOUNTABILITY and discipline begins at the individual level.

BE HONEST WITH YOURSELF about the areas of your life that you're COMFORTABLE in. Surround yourself with people who have the good values and mindsets — they will motivate you and re-focus your ambition.

Scene

16

THE FINAL MOMENT

When Emmett and Avery's airplane landed in South Carolina, they were immediately welcomed by the smell of fresh saltwater in the air as they rushed from the airport to change their clothes for Miss Minnie's dedication event.

When they finally arrived at the event, Emmett, rushing and still in a hurry, almost hit someone in the parking lot with his car as they rushed to grab a parking spot.

"I'm so sorry," He yelled out of the window, after almost hitting a man in a wheelchair.

Avery noticed that the two men were dressed alike, down to the suits, shirts and neckties they wore.

She said, "Matching dress suits, huh? Didn't know it was that type of event."

"You always notice the most random things," Emmett said.

As they rushed into the event in a hurried pace they tried to find a seat before the ceremony began. Again, Emmett almost bumped into two other men who were also dressed alike. They were wearing the same pinstripe suits that the other two guys were wearing.

Huh? Emmett thought to himself.

"Can I help you find your seat?" one of the guys asked.

"Umm, yeah, I'm up front somewhere. My mom's saving seats for us."

As the gentlemen walked them to their seats, he said, "It looks like you're sitting up front where we are."

As they got even closer, Claire Cooper couldn't hold her excitement as she waved from a distance.

The man escorting him to his seats said, "Hey, is that your mom?"

"The crazy lady right there waving?" Emmett asked. "Yep, I belong to her."

The man said, "Wait a minute, are you telling me you're Emmett Cooper, Claire's son?"

"Yes," Emmett responded.

"Wow, look at you all grown up. Man, I can't believe it's you. Did I hear you're at NYU now?"

"Yes I am. I'm sorry but what's your name?"

"My apologies," the man said, "I'm Dorian, Dorian Banks. And this is my son Jordan. It's been a long time since I've seen you, Emmett. I just want you to know how proud we are of you."

We? Emmett thought to himself. *Who is WE? Is this the same Dorian Banks from the story I just read on the airplane?*

Jordan said, "Nice to see you again, Emmett — it looks you're sitting right here up front beside us."

Emmett didn't have time to process the interaction before his mother Claire Cooper jumped into his arms.

"Mom, relax, it's only been a few weeks since I saw you last," Emmett said.

"That's six weeks too long, my darling!" she said with the beaming pride of a mamma bear. "And look at you, Avery, aren't you precious as always. So great to see you!"

"Great to see you too, Claire. We're super excited to meet Miss Minnie — we feel like we know her already!"

Their hugs and greetings were interrupted by the emcee on the microphone as he announced the official start to the evening's dedication event.

"Ladies and gentlemen, I'd like you to help me welcome a man to this stage that has served the low country community for his entire life. Please help me welcome to the stage Pastor Eddie White!"

Avery said, "Look Emmett, that man's name tag says Pastor Eddie. He must be the man who worked with Minnie at the DMV."

As Pastor Eddie took the stage, the audience was packed with hundreds of people who came out to show support for Miss Minnie and her impact on the Clairmont and Charleston community. Others who'd moved out of South Carolina to other parts of the world made the effort to fly back for the event.

Pastor Eddie approached the microphone to officially begin the event.

"I'd like to open the event up in prayer. Dear Lord, we thank you for your son Jesus and the grace that you've given us all. Most especially, we want to thank you for this angel, our sister and friend that we're honoring today. Please continue to bless Miss Minnie with many more years of health, protection and the courage to lead us all in your ways, and continue to bring our community together. In Jesus's name we pray, Amen."

Pastor Eddie continued, "Now, I'd like to welcome to the stage Titus Klayton and his dear friend, Judge Frank Fox."

Avery leaned over to Emmett right away.

She said, "Dear friend? I thought that Titus Klayton and Judge Fox were enemies? Either the story we read wasn't true at all, or a lot has changed in the past twenty years!"

They both looked as Titus Klayton and Judge Frank Fox made their way to the stage.

Avery said. "You do realize that those are the two men you almost hit in the parking lot, right?"

As they walked past Emmett and his mother, Claire said, "Emmett, you're going to love Titus. He's such a great public speaker."

Emmett said, "Why is Judge Fox going to the stage with him?"

Claire reached out and grabbed Titus's hand as he walked by. "You've got this, Titus Klayton — do this one for old man Moscufo," she said.

Titus turned the handshake into a quick hug as he stopped fast enough to greet Claire as he walked by.

Titus said, "What happened to you, Claire? The girls and I saved you a seat over there?"

"Sorry about that, I had to grab these seats because Emmett's plane was running late."

Claire also gave a quick wave to the man in the wheelchair.

"Great to see you, Judge Fox. We love you!" she said, as she kneeled down to hug him in his wheelchair.

Avery said, "Emmett, wait, Titus got his legs back and Judge Fox is now in a wheelchair? Am I seeing this the right way?"

Emmett said, "Either Titus Klayton got his legs back just like he said he would, or we got that whole story completely backwards."

As Titus Klayton and Judge Frank Fox took the stage together, seeing them together was the ultimate sign of human connection and community. Miss Minnie, seated on stage as the guest of honor, couldn't hold back her tears at the sight of the two men joined together.

"I'm so proud of you two," she whispered as Titus began.

Titus grasped the edge of the podium long enough to pause and take in the sights and sounds of a united community. People from all backgrounds had story after story about Miss Minnie's impact on their lives as they passed through the Clairmont DMV for over 40 years.

Titus began by saying, "First, I'd like to acknowledge a very special friend. You all may have noticed that many of the men here are dressed in a very special, tailor-made pinstripe suit today. Other than Miss Minnie, Mr. Joe Moscufo was a large inspiration for many of us in this community to come together again."

Titus gave a special wave to Joe's wife Carol Moscufo, who was seated on the front row.

"Ms. Moscufo, Joe was always here for us, in ways that he never truly had to be — so now that he's gone, we will be the ones who will take care of you."

Their entire audience stood to clap and show their appreciation for Joe Moscufo while many of them took the time to hug Carol.

Claire Cooper and many others couldn't hold back their emotions as they began to cry.

"Joe Moscufo meant the world to me," she whispered to Emmett, as she squeezed his hand.

Titus continued, "We all wore the pinstripe suits today to honor Joe. He never went anywhere without a fresh suit on. He always said it was just a *La Cosa Nostra* thing that we'd never understand."

Jordan Banks yelled from the front row, *"Just like taking a swim with cement shoes,"* and everyone laughed.

Titus finished up by saying, "We are here to celebrate the official name change of the main road that the Clairmont DMV sits on. And before we welcome our the lady of the hour to the stage, I'd like to ask former Judge Frank Fox to share a few words."

Titus slowly wheeled Judge Fox's wheelchair in front of the podium for the audience to see him. After Titus adjusted the microphone for him, Judge Fox took a moment to look into the eyes of everyone in attendance.

"Miss Minnie is a special gift to our world," the judge said. "Because of one special day at her DMV during the Christmas season many years ago, many lives have been changed. Some lives were even saved, and my life was one of those. She taught me about grace and forgiveness in ways that I could never imagine, and it's because of her that a retired judge like me can stand here before you today, standing hand in hand with a gentleman that has become my brother, a man who I once falsely imprisoned for a crime that he did not commit."

Turning around to look at Miss Minnie on stage, Judge Fox said, "Miss Minnie, because of you and your crazy rules at that

DMV... we may have been angry about all of your rules, but the truth is, **the day I put my phone down was the day I picked my life up.** And because of you, the *FR33DOM Innocence Project* that Titus Klayton and I were able to create together has helped to free thousands of men and women who were falsely accused or given excessive prison sentences they didn't deserve, and many of those men and women are here with their families today to show their support for your leadership and the impact that you've made in their lives."

As the formerly imprisoned men and women began to stand up, everyone in attendance erupted with cheers and support. It was a powerful moment for the audience and for Miss Minnie — a lady who was not known for showing emotion. The sight of men and women standing with their families after receiving their freedom was enough to also make Emmett and Avery emotional.

Emmett looked over at Claire and said, "Mom, I'm glad that you made me come to see this. This really is special."

"Of course, son, this is about community," she said.

"And thank you for sending me the story," he said.

"What story?" she responded.

"What do you mean, *what story?*" Emmett said, "I'm talking about THE *story*, Minnie Moments."

Claire still didn't respond.

Emmett grabbed his phone.

After he pulled up the email that Claire sent to him, he said, "This story," as he pointed to the document titled MINNIE MOMENTS.

"Where did you get that from?" his mother screamed.

Emmett stopped right away. He could tell by her body language that something was wrong. Having been raised for over twenty-one years by Claire Cooper, Emmett knew when his mother was mad — *he knew that look.*

He quickly defended himself as he whispered, *"Mom, you're the one who sent this to me, look,"* as he showed her the email address that she sent it from.

After looking at Emmett's phone, Claire realized that she *did* send the email, *by mistake.*

Claire's body began to shake and blood rushed to her face. Out of everything they'd experienced together, even under the threat of a cancer diagnosis, Claire's response was so passively violent on the inside that Emmett couldn't recognize the woman seated next to him on the outside.

Emmett's girlfriend Avery held his arm tightly as she observed the interaction between the mother and son.

Claire sat still for a moment, then finally, with her body still barely able to move or function, Claire found the composure inside of herself to utter four, short words.

"I... wasn't... ready... yet."

The tension between Emmett and his mother Claire Cooper was temporarily suspended by Judge Fox's announcement as he officially introduced the honored guest of the hour to the stage.

It was time for Miss Minnie to be honored.

Titus and Pastor Eddie pushed Miss Minnie's wheelchair to the stage just as they'd previously done for Judge Fox. Once in position, Miss Minnie didn't take take much time to start her speech.

She began by saying, "Many years ago, as a young girl, my heart was in despair because of the condition of humanity. I saw how illusive **love, joy** and **peace** were to many and **patience** and **kindness** were no longer virtuous. **Faithfulness and hopefulness** were slipping out of our grasp, and those who controlled the narrative seemed to no longer care about **gentleness, goodness** and **self-control** — instead choosing fear and division as a means to control others and to satisfy their ambition.

"In a world that felt so big, I was broken-hearted. Until one day, God gave me the strength and the vision to make one decision. Now I stand here today, in the full understanding of truth that God has given to each of us. Now I understand the significance of the two most powerful words that each of you can also choose to use at any moment — and those two words are, *I DECIDED.* Because once you say those two words, everything that you need from that moment on will be yours in full supply.

"When you say the words "I Decided", everything you need from that moment on will be yours, in full supply."

"So... *I DECIDED.* I decided to use the **one opportunity** that I had to connect my head, my heart and my soul with the *courage to change the narrative.* I began with the simplest of rules, rules that as a young girl I was tasked by God to fulfill as a small part of my purpose. And because *I DECIDED*, those rules have influenced each of you that are here today. Those rules have reminded us all that when you choose life, you choose to face the fullness of life's experiences with COURAGE, including the highs and lows and the joy and pain that accompany this great mystery called life. Choosing life also means **choosing to love yourself, and choosing humanity over ambition, choosing humanity over innovation, and choosing humanity over convenience**. And above all, choosing life means choosing to love — **especially when others are in your presence**. Love them completely, free of distraction, and when you do, God will reveal a greater purpose inside of you well. Because your greatest contribution to this world begins with the words, **I DECIDED**."

Miss Minnie took a few moments to catch her breath. In what appeared to be the inevitability of her old age catching up with her, it was much more. She was preparing for her final reveal.

Miss Minnie looked directly at Jordan Banks.

She said, "Mr. Jordan Banks, you **DECIDED** to choose life, by walking out of that bathroom, and because of that decision, you are now changing lives everyday. Your Connections Academy Elementary School has inspired millions around the world."

Miss Minnie looked at Judge Frank Fox. She said, "And the Honorable Judge Frank Fox." She paused. "You **DECIDED** to use past regrets to motivate yourself to invest in the lives of others, and as we look at the audience today, you now have many people waiting for you on the outside of the bathroom door."

Briefly glancing at Titus Klayton, Miss Minnie took a moment to gather herself. She finally said, "Mr. Titus Klayton, or shall I say, Mr. TK..."

The audience lit up with laughter.

"TK, you **DECIDED** to be a shining example... of the most important aspect of humanity, forgiveness. God must be with your soul because **there are many of us who still fail to understand the true power of forgiveness.**"

She paused as she began to wipe tears away from her eyes. Everyone was inspired by Miss Minnie's emotion.

She continued by saying, "TK, many of us here today are blessed to say that we still haven't faced a single ounce of the challenges that you've experienced. That is how I know that God has gifted you with a heart of faithfulness, perseverance and forgiveness. And because you **DECIDED** to share your gifts with others, you have been given the true fullness of freedom that it brings, freedom that even the bars of a jail cell could never take away."

Miss Minnie wiped more tears away.

After she paused, she briefly glanced at Claire Cooper in the audience. Then, she looked at her son Emmett Cooper, with his girlfriend Avery holding his hand. Immediately, Miss Minnie attempted to stand from her wheelchair.

Pastor Eddie grabbed her.

"Miss Minnie, Miss Minnie — are you okay?" he asked.

Pushing Eddie away, she said, "I've been waiting twenty years for this. Please step away and hand me my walker."

Miss Minnie used all of her energy to finally stand up.

She took her first steps towards the edge of the stage as she attempted to walk down the front steps to get close to Claire and Emmett Cooper, where they were seated in the front row.

The moment had come. It was finally time.

Claire Cooper was still shaking from the discovery that she sent the story to her son Emmett by mistake. As Miss Minnie made even stronger eye contact with Claire, her heart began to jump.

It took Miss Minnie a few moments to get through the audience. She finally stood before Claire and Emmett Cooper. After catching her breath, she hesitated briefly — while staring directly into Claire Cooper's eyes.

Miss Minnie said, "Claire Cooper... or shall I call you *Darla DuVernay?*" in a dramatic tone.

Emmett clutched his mothers hand.

Miss Minnie repeated, "Darla DuVernay."

In that exact moment, Emmett reimagined the character from the story he read — the young, pregnant girl in the DMV.

"Darla DuVernay," Minnie said. "From the moment I first met you, I knew you were a star. A real star, with a real purpose. Yessssss. A purpose to shine brightly, to shine for others."

Miss Minnie shifted her focus onto Emmett Cooper.

No longer resisting her emotions, Miss Minnie fought through the tears as she looked directly into Emmett's eyes and said, **"YOUR MOTHER DECIDED... "**

She paused, then she said, "She decided twice."

Never breaking her eye contact with Emmett, she said, "Your mother, Darla DuVernay, she decided to choose life, in the greatest sense of the word."

Everyone in the audience knew what that meant.

Emmett knew EXACTLY what it meant.

As Miss Minnie turned back to Claire, she said, "It was you, Claire Cooper," no longer addressing her as Darla DuVernay.

Claire was stunned.

"Claire Cooper, **YOU DECIDED** to believe. To believe in you. To believe in YOUR life."

Then Miss Minnie placed her hands on Claire's stomach as she said, "And today, it is my greatest hope, that you will continue to believe, and fight, to once again experience the fullness of life in your cancer battle."

Turning away from Claire and Emmett Cooper to address the remaining audience, Miss Minnie said, "Though I stand here with praise from many of you, I stand fully conscious of the burdens of times to come, and even though I stand in despair, I must trust that my contributions were sufficient. Although my flesh wants to see the harvest of seeds planted, I know not. But perhaps in the next world. So **I HAVE DECIDED** to trust that my efforts were sufficient, and the rest of the mystery will surely be fulfilled by the only one who has the power to fulfill such destiny."

As soon as she finished her speech, the audience jumped to their feet as they gave Miss Minnie a standing ovation.

After the conclusion of her speech, many of the attendees stayed for hours after the event to meet Miss Minnie personally and take photographs with her.

Many of the original customers who were at the DMV nearly twenty years ago on that cold December day gathered with each other as they hugged and shared memories.

It was an even more special moment for Emmett, after being raised by Claire as a single mother. That evening represented something much bigger than a dedication event for Miss Minnie. That evening, Emmett Cooper was given the gift of identity. He finally got it. He finally understood the many years of support from *Uncle Joe* and birthday cards from *The Judge and Auntie J* — short for Jaha Fatou. He always thought were distant family that he hadn't met yet.

He was correct, they were family members and much more. They were a village and community that God blessed Claire with that allowed Emmett to grow into the young man that he'd become.

Titus Klayton approached the group as he hugged everyone. He gave an especially warm hug and embrace to Claire before she turned to address Emmett.

"Emmett, as you know, we lost Uncle Joe Moscufo recently. Fortunately, many of us were able to reconnect at his funeral."

Emmett didn't know Titus very well, but he recognized the somewhat nervous look on Titus's face. His mother Claire looked equally nervous as well.

Then Emmett noticed that Titus didn't exactly "step away" from his mother Claire after he hugged her. He embraced her with great affection, for what seemed like… *a long time.*

Claire turned towards Emmett and said, "Son, I want to…"

Emmett interrupted her, as he noticed the nervous look in both of their eyes.

"Mom, the answer is yes. I couldn't think of a man that you deserve to have in your life more than Titus Klayton. You both deserve each other — I'd be honored."

Claire was stunned.

Claire looked at Titus and said, "Well, that didn't go like we planned."

Miss Minnie said, "Ummm humm, it didn't take a mystery to figure that out. You two been staring and smiling at each other all day long."

Then Miss Minnie announced, "If ya'll need me for anything else, I will be volunteering down at the **Connections Academy** from now on."

She continued, "After Jordan started that school, it's so popular that they have a five-year waiting list for kids who want to go there." As she looked at Jordan Banks.

Jordan said, "Oh stop it, Miss Minnie, I didn't build the school by myself. Where do you think we came up with the name in the first place," as he patted her on the back with pride.

She said, "I can't wait to start volunteering at that school. Somebody has to teach those kids how to act like human beings and put those phones down!" Everyone laughed!

Then Jordan reached over to place his hands on Judge Fox's shoulder. He said, "Well, we couldn't have built the school without a lot of political help from our community," as he rubbed Judge Fox's shoulders.

Then, Titus Klayton join in, "You also couldn't have done it without the personal and corporate contributions of one of the fastest-growing female CEOs in the country," as he hugged Claire Cooper.

Claire blushed as she said, "I learned a long time ago what my job really was as a business leader. My job was to create a place where my team could focus, without distractions, where they felt connected to each other as a team — *the rest of the mystery was up to…*"

Miss Minnie interrupted. "Listen, y'all started all these schools and successful businesses using all of my leadership philosophies, so now, y'all must pay me for using my strategies! I think five-percent royalty fees will do just fine!" As she reached her hands out to collect the payment.

The End

TO MY GIRLS:

"Lisa, Dori, LiLi and Harley.
Thank You For Disrupting Me."

AFTERWORD

Each of the characters in this story had a specific role to play — *and so do you*. Many people, families, teams and organizations throughout the world have used the **Disruption Model** to spark challenging conversations and get honest about getting better. So remember:

> You must continue to **DISRUPT YOURSELF.**
> You must become more **DISCIPLINED.**
> You must get **UNCOMFORTABLE.**
> You must create greater **HUMAN CONNECTION.**

A business leader once said to me, "Morris, I worked hard for my entire life to be successful and find comfort, so why would I disrupt everything now?"

I said, "The problem is, your success is all about you. But if you find the courage to **DISRUPT YOURSELF,** you will inspire everyone else around you, to get better." Because…

The greatest **parents** do it every **day**…
The greatest **teams** do it every **year**…
The greatest **leaders** do it every **moment**…
They **DISRUPT THEMSELVES**, to grow.

Thank you for reading!

Morris Morrison